How Close We Come

WARNER BOOKS

A Time Warner Company

This book is a work of fiction. Names, characters, places and incidents either are the product of the author's imagination or used fictitiously, and any resemblance to actual persons, living or dead, events, or locales is entirely coincidental.

This Warner Books edition is published by arrangement with Banks Channel Books
Warner Books, Inc., 1271 Avenue of the Americas, New York, NY 10020

Visit our Web site at http://warnerbooks.com

 A Time Warner Company

Printed in the United States of America

First Warner Books Printing: September 1998

10 9 8 7 6 5 4 3 2 1

Library of Congress Cataloging-in-Publication Data

Kelly, Susan S.
    How close we come : a novel of women's friendships / Susan S. Kelly.
        p. cm.
    ISBN 0-446-52418-2
    1. Female friendship—Fiction. 2. Custody of children—Fiction.
    3. Women—Fiction. I. Title.
    PS3561.E39716H68   1998
    813'.54—DC21   98-14343
                                                            CIP

To Sterling, for push and praise

God instructs the heart, not by ideas but by pains and contradictions.

Jean-Pierre de Caussade

J. D. Salinger
Franny & Zooey

How Close We Come

$\mathscr{C}$ hapter 1

No contest for *my* husband," Ruth said. "Reed's all-time favorite scene is the cowboys farting around the campfire in *Blazing Saddles*."

I laughed. Side by side across my bed, Ruth and I were mourning the death and dearth of Great Cathartic Scenes in Recent American Cinema, but had gotten derailed in predicting our husbands' hypothetical picks.

"Scotty's would have to be . . ." I mused, tapping my fingers against my rib cage, "the Saint Crispin's Day speech from *Henry V*. 'We few, we happy few.' "

"I know, I know, Larry Olivier waxing eloquently about holding his manhood dear." Ruth rolled her eyes at me. They were raccoon-rimmed with brown shadow and feathery, erratic streaks of black where her daughter's aim with the mascara wand had erred.

My own four-year-old, Bethie, padded back to my

side clutching bobbie pins and barrettes in her chubby fingers, as well as a baby hairbrush, whose soft, pliable bristles, useless as new grass, she pressed against my scalp.

"Or the universal default for most men, I'd bet," Ruth continued, "the hospital scene from *Brian's Song.*" She lowered her voice, aiming for husky emotion but achieving only hilarious throaty gruffness. " 'I *love* Brian Piccolo.' "

"You are terrible." I laughed. "Okay, where were we? *Kramer vs. Kramer.*"

"Close, but no cigar. Lacks that one wrencher scene."

"Not even in the courtroom?"

Sloan yanked at her mother's hair. "You have a rat's nest, Mommy," she said.

"Ouch!" Ruth winced.

We were lying across my wide queen-sized bed, though it wasn't broad enough to prevent our legs from sticking awkwardly over at the side. Scotty was campaigning for a king mattress, but I was opposed, and cited Ruth as an ally. ("God," she'd agreed, "they're so vulgar-looking. Like having a trampoline in your bedroom.") The horizontal position of our bodies allowed our hair to fall conveniently over the edge of the bed so that Bethie and Sloan could comb and braid and part it, playing Beauty Parlor. It was a favorite game for all four of us, one we often resorted to on rainy afternoons. Even at their young age the girls were already savvy to the pointlessness of working puzzles or building wooden block villages: sooner or later the puzzles and blocks had to be knocked down, taken apart, and cleaned up. I don't know where the boys were; probably holding farting contests of their own. Both seven, my son, Jay, and Ruth's Grayson were ripe for bathroom humor. The day before, giggling and thyroid-eyed with suppressed glee, they'd summoned their younger sisters into the bathroom to witness a foot-long turd Jay had deposited in the toilet. They'd gotten the disgusted reaction they'd hoped for, and twenty-five minutes of punishment in time-out as well.

"*Summer of '42*," I proposed.

"Oh, absolutely. Hymie at the window when she reads the telegram. Oldie but goodie. Obscure but not forgotten. *Steel Magnolias*."

I frowned, but Ruth protested. "No fair disqualifying something just because it wasn't a darling of the critics or doesn't meet your superior literary standards."

"Okay, you include *Kramer* and I'll let *Magnolias* pass."

"Hold still, Mommy," Bethie commanded. Along with our hair styling came makeovers, compliments of eyeshadow, blush, and "lipcolor" department store freebies. The first time we'd played Beauty Parlor, I stood up and greeted myself in the mirror: blue shadow high as my eyebrows, perfect circles of red on my cheeks, a lipsticked mouth in clown proportions. A dozen primary-colored plastic barrettes were clamped close to my scalp and forehead. "It's worse than inadvertently catching sight of yourself in that mirrored strip above the meat bin at the supermarket," Ruth had said. But Sloan and Bethie had been delighted with their cosmetology results.

Our hair would be greasy tangled messes when the girls finished our "appointments," but the game would have served its purpose—entertainment for the children, relative peace for us. And Ruth and I were doing what we liked best too: talking. As I miss Ruth, I miss those afternoon sessions, the tender tiny fingers of our daughters, whose clumsy touch was as soothing and relaxing as any skillful masseuse's. My hair was, is, thick and heavy, but never styled—a result, I always claim, of having somehow missed that stage of adolescence when girls spend hours mirror-bound, figuring out how to use hot combs and round brushes and blow dryers to their best advantage. Versed in Gail Sheehy, Ruth always held that if you skip a stage in life you'll have to return to it sooner or later, though I never asked her if the theory applied to grooming. I do own a hot comb, actually, stashed in the medicinal netherworld beneath the bathroom sink. The first time I tried to use the fiery wand I burned my neck so badly that it looked as though I had a hickey, and I was forced to wear a turtleneck to a no-excuses vestry function with Scotty even though it was April.

"Mom," Bethie complained. "I can't braid your hair. It's not long enough."

I pointed to my navel. "I used to have hair down to here."

"No you did not," Bethie countered with severe, run-on authority.

"Get that tall green book from the bottom bookshelf in the den and I'll prove it."

"Cheater," Ruth said. Useless errands were another acknowledged time-wasting ploy.

Bethie returned with the leather volume, fanning its black-and-white pages. Ruth rolled over. "What *is* this?"

"High school yearbook."

"Called '*Quair*'? I'm afraid to ask."

" 'Little book' in Latin."

"Naturally. Why hadn't I thought of that?"

I flipped through pictures of athletic teams and volunteer organizations until I reached the senior pictures. "There," I said to Bethie, pointing to myself. My straight hair hung like a curtain to my waist. "Told you so. Nannie nannie boo boo."

"Is that you?" Bethie squealed appreciatively.

Ruth sidled next to her, ignoring Sloan's indignant "I'm not done yet!"

" 'Finished' yet," Ruth corrected. "Wow," she said. "You *did* have some lengthy tresses."

"I was convinced that if I cut it, my personality would vanish too. It took me until my junior year in college to work up the nerve. And only then, I might add, because I was secure that Scotty sufficiently adored me to risk cutting off ten inches."

"And?"

"He didn't even notice."

Ruth ran her finger along the quotation beneath my name, reading aloud. " '*The quiet watcher, observer always, in solitary shaded shadows.*' Shaded shadows? Did you make this up?"

"Of course not; give me a little creative credit. It was the yearbook editor's idea of sensitive haiku. Summing me up in ten words or less."

"Ah, the soulful, sensitive seventies. But it's not bad," Ruth mused. "You *are* a watcher."

Still on my back, I peered closely at her, gauging my reaction to her statement, her judgment.

"See?" Ruth said gently, deflecting. "You're at it again. Watching me." She let pages drift through her fingers, stopping finally at a two-page spread on the Danish exchange student. "Looks like the alien Pia was spared the haiku dictum. She picked her own quote. '*Don't you know that people change, thus relationships change, and that pain is a sign of changes, not endings?*' " she read.

"Turn back over, Mommy!" Sloan yelled.

"*Please,*" Ruth responded automatically.

"Didn't you have yearbook quotes in the sixties?" I asked.

"I refuse to answer on the grounds that it may incriminate me as a dork." The girls tittered. At last, a conversation they could comprehend. Grimacing, Ruth confessed. " 'I am a part of all that I have met.' "

I howled. "Let me guess. You also had a poster on

your wall that said, 'If you love something, let it go, and if it returns it is yours' superimposed on a deserted beach."

"Actually," Ruth said, "I had a poster illustrating all the positions for"—she cut her eyes toward our juvenile hairstylists—"intercourse, corresponding to each astrological sign. In black light neons." A fresh torrent of rain pelted against the windowpane. She sat up. "God. 'The sun did not shine. It was too wet to play.'"

"I know, I know," Bethie crowed. "*Cat in the Hat.* 'So we sat inside that cold cold wet day.' Can we get a kitten, Mommy?"

"No. They eat the birds."

Ruth flopped back down and tapped a comb against my rib cage. "Now, where were we? *Splendor in the Grass.*"

"*Funny Girl.*"

"*Ordinary People.*"

"*Camelot.* When Guinevere is leaving for the nunnery, and her nose is running, and she says, 'Arthur, so many times I've looked into your eyes and seen love there.'" I sniffed sympathetically.

"*Prince of Tides.*"

"*The King and I.*"

"'He may not always be,'" Ruth warbled, "'what you would have him be, then all at once he'll do, something wonderful.' Don't you say that line to yourself at least once every day?" Sloan dropped an elastic to clap her hands over her ears. I laughed again. "Your turn," Ruth said.

I considered a minute. "Can we count made-for-TV movies?"

"Depends."

I whistled a tune inexpertly, and though I botched the haunting strains, it was melody enough.

"Ahh," Ruth said softly, and sighed. "Meggie. Poor Meggie. Poor Ralph. Poor Father deBricassart. Yes. That counts." She cradled her head in her palm. "You know why we love *The Thorn Birds*, Pril? I'll tell you why we love it. Because it's about yearning for and lusting after something you can never ever have. Denial. What a theme. Nobody gets the priest. The sperm but not the soul." She sighed again. "Let's do some subcategories. Cathartic superlatives. Saddest death."

I heard the refrigerator slam. Jay and Grayson, foraging for food less than an hour after lunch. "Hey, Mom!" Grayson yelled upstairs. "I thought you were going to make meringues for us today!"

"Can't make meringues on rainy days!" Ruth hollered back.

"Why not?"

"They won't rise."

"Why?"

Ruth exhaled a noisy sigh. "Ready?" she asked me. "Because I said so!" we sang out on cue. Without missing a beat, she continued: "*Out of Africa.*"

"Are you sure?"

"You got a sadder death?"

"Promise not to laugh."

Ruth widened her eyes and mouth in feigned innocence. "Have I ever laughed at you?"

"*Love Story.*"

She giggled. "My. I don't believe I'da tole that. Ali McGraw was wooden, but Pinocchio was a better actor."

"After I saw *Love Story* I bought a little knitted cloche so I could look like Jenny and have someone who looked like Ryan O'Neal fall in love with me." I shook my head. "New category: biggest sob. And I know mine."

"Which?"

"Heard of Loew's Grand Theater in Atlanta?"

"Sure. The premiere of *Gone With the Wind.*"

"One afternoon in January while I was being paid to summarize depositions, I stood for four hours at my thirtieth-story window and watched Loew's Grand burn to cinders. There was nothing firefighters could do. It was terrible, watching that grand old lady die. Such an ignoble demise." I stared at the ceiling. "Scotty estimates that I've spent one hundred twenty-six hours of my life watching *Gone With the Wind.*" I sensed Ruth's smile beside me. "The next morning on the way to work, my bus passed what was left of Loew's Grand, nothing but charred, cindery black stalks behind yellow police ribbons. The rubble was still smoking, with long icicles hanging from the charred beams where dripping water had frozen overnight. Then I threw up."

"On the bus?"

"Right there in the middle of the aisle. Scotty blamed it on the overheated bus, stinking of sausage biscuits, cheap perfume, and exhaust. I thought it was the sight of that pathetic, burned-out shell of a building." I looked at Ruth. "But I was just pregnant."

"Just," Ruth enunciated dryly.

Sloan interrupted, shoving an eyeshadow container before Ruth's nose. "What's the name of this color?"

Ruth squinted. " 'Innocent Blue.' Geez."

"Geez, what?" Sloan said, stroking the powder from her mother's eye to temple. Ruth looked like a Cleopatra clone who hadn't slept for a week.

I fell silent, remembering my lingering melancholy for the vanished theater, and what it represented. Scotty had tried to understand my sorrow. And failed. Such attachment escaped him.

The sound of bickering erupted from Jay's room. He and Grayson were fighting over who deserved to be the Architect in a game of Life. "Now, *that's* pathetic," Ruth said. "Two seven-year-olds who already know which career card in Life produces the highest salary. Quiet!" she barked. Sensing more interesting commotion down the hall, and nurturing a futile hope that the boys would let them join their game, Bethie and Sloan skittered from the bedroom. *"Casablanca."*

"West Side Story."

"Love in the Afternoon," Ruth suddenly said.

"Oh, Audrey imploring Gary at the train station! Every Audrey Hepburn movie."

10

"But we've left out *numero uno*, the all-time weeper great. Or just saved it for last."

I watched her pull a skewed barrette from her hair, and knew. "*The Way We Were*. At the end, when Katie and Hubbel accidentally meet outside the Plaza. When she brushes Hubbel's bangs out of his eyes, like she'd done a thousand times before. Then."

Ruth shook her head. "No, no, no. It's when Katie says, 'Wouldn't it be lovely to go back the way we were, when everything was easy?' And Hubbel says, 'Oh, Katie, it was never easy.' "

"No, no. It's the scene when he says, 'You want too much!' and Katie says, 'Oh, but look at what I've got.' "

One by one, I unclipped the diminutive barrettes from my hair. "You know what?" Ruth said, her painted lips twisted in a rueful smile. "It's the women we cry for in all those movies. Jenny and Katie and Meggie and Anna and the rest. Ever noticed? The women, always the women." She curved herself close and cozy and fetal, and pulled a small pillow beneath her head, a baby gift whose creweled linen pillow slip hadn't looked crisp since the moment I'd opened it. "Do you see the common thread in all these cathartic scenes?" she asked me. "Don't you see what happens in every one, Pril? They're all about departing. About leaving. About separating. Those are the stories that make us cry. They're the only stories worth telling, or writing, or reading, or watching. Worth remember-

11

ing." We lay there, curled and stilled, until shrieks snatched us back.

"Mommy! Grayson put shredlocks on my Barbie! He ruined my Totally Hair Barbie!"

"*Dread*locks," came Grayson's withering reply. "Dreadlocks, dummy."

"He called me a dummy!"

And so Ruth and I, mothers, rose reluctantly to intervene and mediate. Behind us on the quilted white coverlet were left the faint impressions of our bodies, and smudges of Innocent Blue.

It is laughable now, the Beauty Parlor game, our list of movies that dreary, rainy afternoon. Laughable and ludicrous that we cried or agonized over scenes and plots and characters meaningless beyond what they had once meant to us, during some bygone phase of our lives.

But there's another movie I'll forever associate with Ruth, though not for its story. It fits her formula, consists almost entirely of departures and separations. But it's a mere line of *Dr. Zhivago* that captures my intricate, indissoluble connection to Ruth. Whenever I think of movies, of the two of us together, and of Ruth now alone, that spare single line comes back to me: *"I suppose I was a little in love with her myself."*

Chapter 2

In what capacity do you know the defendant, Mrs. Henderson?"

"We were neighbors."

"And are you still neighbors?"

"Yes."

" 'Yes'? " he repeated sarcastically.

"The Campbells still live beside us, yes."

Annoyed with the response, the prosecutor rearranged his tie with exaggerated precision. "So I presume your friendship with Mrs. Campbell dates from the time you and your husband moved to Greensboro, North Carolina?"

"No."

Not the expected answer. It threw him. " 'No'? " he echoed, the hollow vowel rising an octave.

"No."

Susan S. Kelly

"Then just how long have you known the defendant, Mrs. Campbell?"

"Since . . . since we were children."

Across the expanse of tile floor, Ruth bowed her head and smiled.

She didn't remember me, but I remembered her. We hadn't officially met yet. Our driveways were parallel, separated by a slowly disintegrating split-rail fence. Still, I knew there were children next door. On the kitchen windowsill I'd glimpsed a medicine bottle with unmistakable pink contents: amoxycillin for earaches and strep, childhood's winter ailments. Like me, my neighbor evidently never finished a prescription once the symptoms were relieved and the children quit complaining. Too, the usual assortment of faded, forgotten riding toys were strewn near the back entrance, waiting for spring.

It was early February, freezing, and we'd been living in, if not entirely *moved* in, our house for two weeks. Scotty believed post-Christmas real estate carried the best prices, when owners were desperate for cash and their yards looked the worst. I'd dragged the children all over Greensboro that day buying maddening necessities: picture, closet, and shower curtain hooks, wide-bottomed lightbulbs for the front sconces, extension cords, odd-sized batteries for the smoke alarms, endless widgets. But I'd forgotten milk. Mundane milk for mundane macaroni. I gathered up a coatless, year-old Bethie, ignoring her "wanna walk" kicked protests,

14

called Jay, and trudged next door on the time-honored errand of borrowing.

Though every window blazed with light, no one answered my knock. Bethie whimpered with cold. I pushed, and the door opened. "Hello?" I called. "Anybody home?"

"Heyyo?" Bethie lisped, echoing my greeting.

No one was fixing supper in the kitchen, littered with the recognizable wreckage of family, of children. Miniature robots, crayons, and Big Gulp soda cups in which cigarette butts floated competed for counter space. Crumpled jackets and muddy boots were scattered on shiny vinyl floor tiles whose squares formed an incomplete crossword puzzle over plywood sub-flooring. We walked down a hardwood hallway coated with a fine silt of white dust. Sheetrocked walls on either side were patched with spackle splotches.

"It stinks in here," Jay said.

"It's the construction." But there was another, stronger smell: smoke.

"I hear people back there," he said, and pointed to a closed door at the end of the hall.

"Sounds like a television."

"See, they get to watch, Mom," he immediately whined, protesting a new rule I was unsuccessfully trying to enforce at Scotty's insistence. "Easy for you to dictate," I'd said. "You're not here. You don't have to make them obey it. I have to be the bad guy."

As we approached, the smell of smoke, of fire, grew so pervasive that panic seized me. Acting purely on in-

15

stinct, I flung open the door. But no heart-pounding, terror-filled inferno lay within; instead the scene that greeted us could have been lifted directly from the Keystone Cops.

Naked but for a towel bunched at her stomach, a woman was sitting cross-legged at the foot of the bed. A preschool boy and baby girl flanked her, naked too but for underpants and diaper, their legs dangling against the pleated dust ruffle. All three were rapt before a television screen two feet away from their faces. Absorbed in Disney's *Sleeping Beauty*, they were utterly oblivious of the gray clouds of smoke billowing from the fireplace across the room, and a thin stream of water flowing from an adjoining bathroom and pooling on the bedroom floor.

"Your damper . . ." I started. "The water . . ." Six eyes turned in my direction.

"Oh my God!" the woman shrieked, and leaped from the bed. She dashed across the room, slipping in the puddled water, and fumbled through the acrid haze with a poker.

"Mommy's mooning!" the boy crowed. The metal damper cover clanked open.

"Shit," the woman muttered under her breath, and hopped comically, breasts bouncing, toward the bathroom and the overflowing tub. She reached around the open door, found a robe on a hook, and ineffectively wrapped it around her. "Cripes!" she added for emphasis. "Start the bath, start the fire, start the movie, and forget. *Mea culpa.*" She ran her hands through her dark hair and, looking at me, shrugged. "What can I say? We love this part of the movie." I took in the fine features, the bisque skin, her lazy beauty. Ruth always seemed a living, breathing Ralph Lauren advertisement, and even bulkily clothed in terry cloth she looked every inch a model.

Still on the bed, the dark-eyed baby girl began to warble along with the video. " 'I know you, I danced with you once upon a dream.' "

Bethie wiggled out of my arms and toddled over to the bed. "Up wif!" she demanded.

"Neither flood nor fire interrupts *Sleeping Beauty*," the woman said. She opened a window, sending a draft of frigid air through the room, then walked over to me and stuck out her hand. "Under the circumstances I should introduce myself. Ruth Campbell."

"Pril Henderson. From next door."

"Oh, sure! I got a card from the real estate sharks, asking that I go over and do the welcome bit, but . . . well, sorry, fresh out of homemade bread." She laughed. "But then, I always *am* fresh out of homemade bread. Pril. For . . . ?"

"Priscilla."

"Right, of course." She squinted at me. "Have all mothers grown to look alike to me, or do I know you from somewhere?"

I hesitated, wondering if Ruth Campbell could place us in past history. I didn't have to squint at her to remember, despite the twenty years since I'd seen her. She was hardly changed from the Paradise girl I'd revered from afar at summer camp, when she was Ruth Sloan. It wasn't that Ruth enjoyed any specific fame at Camp Kiahwassee. Or notoriety. It was simply . . . stature. Every older camper—the girls assigned to Paradise, the two-story barnlike structure in the far wooded reaches of camp acreage—carried a particular cachet. They were the undisputed queens of Kiahwassee, an entitlement of sheer age. It was understood the Paradise girls had bathrooms in their cabin rather than the communal toilets and lavatories we younger campers groped toward in black midnights and chilly mornings. They were allowed relaxed lights-out regulations, stereos, late-night pizzas from town, and other rumored, undreamed-of privileges that boggled our minds. Only Paradise girls were entrusted to hold the paper-collared candles during Sunday night powwows. As we trudged single file to our dark cabins, the Paradise girls sang a mournful taps in clear, harmonious unity, raising the hairs on my arms and threatening me with the only ache of homesickness I ever suffered.

But Ruth Sloan stood apart even from this privileged company. A natural leader, she was yearly elected Chief of the Chippewas, one of three competing tribes to which every camper belonged. A seven-summer veteran of Kiahwassee, Ruth Sloan claimed nearly every counselor as a personal friend. And she came for the entire ten weeks of summer rather than a single session, a fact that incurred whispered suggestions that her parents hated her, shipped her off. Ruth hailed from Charleston and, like the campers from Jacksonville and Birmingham and Atlanta and Memphis, was bestowed automatically with superiority based purely on an out-of-state hometown. Those girls always managed to arrive at camp first, via plane, dibbing the best bunks and the preferred activities, already friendly with each other. But Ruth's trunk came by car, by trailer actually, horse trailer. For Ruth was a rider, and each summer she brought her own horse to camp.

Either Ruth Sloan was exempt from the hated schedule sheets we were required to fill out and mail home as proof of well-rounded participation and accomplishment, or she was a practiced liar. Ruth virtually lived at the stables, cohort and contemporary to the riding instructors. At meals, chapel, morning assembly, she was always dressed for riding, her thighs bound tightly in jodhpurs, the real things, not blue jeans, and beautiful, knee-high black leather boots like a second skin, rather than the clumsy, clomping, black-and-white "fairy stomper" saddle shoes I wore to ride. A velvet helmet framed her freckled nose and escaping curls of her Hayley Mills *Parent Trap* pixie haircut I was dying for. Chatting, laughing, completely at ease with herself and those in authority, she was a combination of horsey earthiness, physical beauty, and athletic grace. In the same way that our age difference of a mere five years was equal to light-years, so was mere envy too remote to define my feelings for Ruth Sloan.

I would see her at the stables when I was there, timidly seeking out the gentlest, most reliably slow

19

horse, but with my mother's words ringing in my ears: "Now don't go to camp and spend all your time in the crafts cabin. Do the things you can't do here. Riflery, and horseback riding, and canoeing." My mother knew me well, knew that I gravitated toward the Nature Shack and its peaceful enterprises of feeding squirrels or catching orange newts whose sticky webbed toes clung to my palm; toward the quiet, focused sport of archery, or the diligent search for fifty arrowheads, enough to win myself a beautiful merit badge woven of bright silken threads. Every day I attended the creative writing hour in the high-ceilinged assembly hall redolent of wood smoke and presided over by a gray-headed, bespectacled counselor inexplicably named Rat.

Now, twenty years later, I smiled at Ruth Sloan Campbell through the smoky haze of her bedroom. "You do know me from somewhere," I said. "From Kiahwassee."

A grin shot across her face. "Kiahwassee! When?" she demanded. "How long did you go?"

"Three summers. Sixty-five through sixty-eight."

"But . . . you must be a lot younger than I am."

"Thirty."

"Thirty-five." She gestured to the children, our girls absorbed in *Sleeping Beauty*, the boys vanished beneath the bed. "Reed and I started late." Her face fell. "Have you heard that they're going to raze the entire camp to develop condos?"

I shook my head.

"But I knew everybody," she said, with no trace of braggadocio. "It's odd that I don't remember you. Who else was in your cabin?"

"Robin Jackson, Alice Swearingham, Berta somebody, and . . ." I trailed off, reluctant even twenty years later to say the name, but recalling it as easily as Ruth's: Polly Franklin, pasty and plump, with growing-out bangs slicked back in a toothed plastic hairband so they stood up around her face like an electrified aureole. "Polly Franklin."

Ruth's expression was stricken. " 'Poor Polly'?" I nodded. Though we'd hardly exchanged two dozen words, Ruth spoke as if we'd been intimate since childhood. "There's always a victim, isn't there?" she said sadly. "Deserved or undeserved, whether a victim of people or of circumstance."

All campers were required to brush their teeth before going to breakfast, but Polly had objected the very first morning. "I can't," she said. "It makes me throw up if I brush my teeth before I eat." We cast knowing looks between ourselves at this patent lie fabricated to let her stay in bed longer. The counselor hadn't fallen for Polly's plaintive excuse either, and marched her to the long tin trough sink with the rest of us at 7:15. The water thundered like Niagara from a dozen spigots as we leaned over, clutching misshapen tubes of Crest and Fruit Stripe.

Suddenly Berta yelled, "Gross me out! She's upchucking out her nose!"

Instantly, two dozen ten-year-olds backed away, giv-

21

ing wide berth to the freak show at the sink. Polly hadn't lied. The toothbrush still jutted from her lips; gluey threads of snot and saliva and toothpaste and vomit streamed from her nostrils. The counselor stepped forward and pulled the toothbrush from Polly's mouth, gently instructing her to wash her face and go back to the cabin to get cleaned up.

After that, Polly was permitted to miss part of first period to return to the cabin and brush her teeth. But she was indelibly marked, singled out in no less public a fashion than if her name had been listed with the top archers and riflists and riders and canoers on Awards Night. "Poor Polly," she became known, a mean moniker of humiliation and derision and pity.

But though she was unaware of it, Polly had subtle, unintentional revenge. Every Sunday night powwow I sat among the flame-flushed faces around the tribal bonfire and listened to the Director read *The Log*, Kiahwassee's weekly creative writing journal, praying fiercely that something I had written and labored over would be selected for reading, and reassuring myself that it was my younger age, not my questionable talent, that prevented my inclusion. And every Sunday night, though I had never seen her darken the door of Rat's sessions, Poor Polly Franklin had a piece read aloud to the impressed assembly of Tribes. She wrote the brief, haunting entries in private, dropped them off, and was accepted. No one needed to teach Poor Polly how to write, or what to say.

"Yes, she was a victim," I agreed with Ruth. The following summer, Poor Polly Franklin hadn't returned to camp. She was Kiahwassee's victim. Not a victim of flood, or crime, or of poverty; but of people. In a way all of us have been. "Yes," I said again.

Ruth glanced at the children and put her finger to her lips. "Shhh. The rug-rat ankle-biter curtain-climbers are temporarily subdued." She steered me toward the kitchen. "Sit," she ordered, reaching in the refrigerator. "Not so much as a peanut for hors d'oeuvres, but I do have wine. Join me?"

I thought only fleetingly of Scotty, who would be home soon, and nodded, removing a Nerf Frisbee from a chair.

"Here," Ruth said, "you have everything there is to know of my life, the proverbial open book." She swept her arm around the chaos, the detritus of family, of off-spring. "Two children, one husband—Ruth 'n' Reed—catchy, no? enduring each other plus the woes, throes, and squalor of renovation. Talk," she commanded, "while I fix leftover medley for dinner. Tell me everything about you."

And so we talked, the five years of age and twenty years of time between us melted and mitigated by children and marriage and history. I drank and watched and listened as talented, lovely, disheveled Ruth Sloan Campbell shredded cheese and beat eggs and reheated roasted potatoes. That is where they eventually found us, Bethie and Sloan, Jay and Grayson, Reed and Scotty. We'd temporarily forgotten them, children and husbands: the necessary addenda of our lives.

Chapter 3

That dusky evening was the first and final instance I ever knocked on Ruth's door. Knocking is for strangers and for salesmen and for children when their parents' door is closed. And never once did Ruth knock on mine.

Without greeting or any other preamble, she strode into my kitchen the following morning, replaced Bethie's stick-figure drawing under a refrigerator magnet with a sheet of notepad paper, and announced, "Info essentials." I set down my mug and read the printed heading: MAGNIFICENTLY UNPREPARED FOR THE LONG LITTLENESS OF LIFE.

"That's essential info too," Ruth said wryly, "but mostly I mean the list underneath. Barber, doctors, dry cleaner, honest mechanic, seamstress, plumber, Chinese and pizza take-outs, and as a bonus the well-kept secret telephone number of a woman who bakes the

24

best caramel cakes in the state. If you're an extra-good girl, I'll follow up with baby-sitters." She winked, then sighed. "When I find some."

I found them, on the sly. I cruised nearby high school and city bus stops clumped with waiting teenagers and housekeepers, and conducted instant on-site interviews with anyone who looked honest, or animated, or took more than a passing interest in Jay and Bethie behind me, car seat captives. The following Thursday, I called Ruth.

"Bring the kids over. Let's go to a two o'clock movie."

"Certainly, Pril, whatever you say. Right after I finish picking money off the tree and jetting off to Barbados. They're all related: as in impossible."

"I've got a daytime sitter."

"You lie."

"No lie."

There was a silence. Then, "Middle-of-the-day movie? I've never heard of anything so decadent in my life. I have a thousand errands I should run instead."

"Of course you do. Just like you will tomorrow. You know what, Ruth? You don't give yourself permission. Do it. Go ahead and give yourself permission to check out for two hours."

I felt the stretch of her smile through the line. "We'll be right over."

The phrase became a kind of mantra for us, applicable to a wide variety of situations. "I'm giving myself permission to buy raspberries out of season." "I'm giving myself permission to postpone dinner to finish this book." "I'm giving myself permission to not change the sheets on the regular day." "I'm giving myself permission to get tipsy tonight." The irony strikes me now, of Ruth giving herself that ultimate permission.

Much of those early days of our friendship was based on the transfer of information. Not only "essential info" about telephone numbers necessary for day-to-day suburban survival; but about who we were, and what we thought, and how we came to be and think that way. Never did I feel indebted to Ruth for the myriad of favors and moving-in kindnesses. She wasn't constructed that way. Yet were she here to ask, I could readily walk through my house and point out the precise pictures she helped me hang, the particular pieces of furniture we dragged from room to room in rearrangement. "Time-out," she groaned. "I think I'm getting a hernia."

"I don't think so," I said skeptically. "Not unless you've suddenly changed genders." Our friendship was lucky, or determined, or fated. We bypassed the awkwardnesses—shy reticence and cautious reserve, interpretations of nuance, hesitations and testings and back-and-forth invitations—of casual or tentative acquaintances. The link between us expanded swiftly, happily, and effortlessly beyond niceties to devotion.

"Be outside at five A.M. tomorrow morning," Ruth

warned me one afternoon three weeks after I'd rescued her from fire and flood.

"Ruth, I like you a lot, but don't push it. We're nowhere near the I'll-do-anything-for-you stage."

"Trust me."

"That's what they all say, horny lovers and drilling dentists and other not-to-be-trusted no-goods."

"It's the cost of quiet, the price of peace. Trust me."

I did. She roused me for the nursery school sign-up, an annual, brutal, first-come first-served ordeal that required planning, cunning, and the willingness to stand in line with fifty other females on a sidewalk outside a low-slung cinderblock church parish hall in frigid predawn darkness. Like a team of harnessed packhorses, we stamped our feet and eyed each other nervously with the whites of our eyes showing in the headlights of cars left running. In the name of available preschool slots we were transformed from fellow nurturers into competitors: mother vs. mother. For not the last time in my life I appreciated how young children simply sock the peer who brazenly breaks in line.

"If I'd really been a friend, I'd have advised you to go ahead and join the church," Ruth murmured at my side. "Members get priority. But you didn't look like the hypocritical type."

"I appreciate the compliment. Are you a member of this church?"

"Depends on your definition of 'member.' Our name is on the roll somewhere, yes. But I've nearly quit going. The whole patriarchal structure of the church *and* the liturgy irks me."

I didn't question her comment, that intimation of the future; I was too surprised by what I'd suddenly realized. "So Grayson's already enrolled? Why are you here, then?"

"Strictly *pour vous*, honey. I told you, the peace that passeth all understanding." She steered me forward. We were nearly to the card table where the precious index cards were stacked, alphabetized, and presided over. "Once one child is in, siblings are automatic. For life or kindergarten graduation, whichever comes first," Ruth explained. We climbed back into the car, hands stuffed into our sweatshirted armpits. "Can Scotty pour cereal?" she asked with monotoned gravity. But a smile played around her mouth.

"Last time I checked he could," I answered, thinking of my mother, whose hated question I'd recently been dismayed to find myself asking my own family: "Are your arms broken?"

"Good," Ruth replied, and instead of home, she drove us to Breakfastown. Inside, the small restaurant was as welcoming and comforting as cinnamon toast, buttery yellow, warm and moist and close with the bustle of activity. We ordered biscuits and coffee and juice at the counter.

"Where you been, Ruth?" the round-faced cashier demanded jovially.

"Changing diapers. Eating bonbons."

The woman laughed, big breasts shaking beneath her apron bib.

"They know your name?" I asked with amazement as we slid into the slick vinyl booth.

"Friends in high places." Ruth shrugged, ripping open a sugar packet. "And low. When I was pregnant, I spent more time in here getting carbo fixes than I did at home. I craved something hot and doughy the entire nine months. Make that eighteen." She bit into the steaming, jelly-slathered biscuit. "Yum," she said between mouthfuls, and tapped my Styrofoam cup with hers. "Cheers."

Within the week of our shivered predawn sign-up, the changeability of March weather asserted itself; Greensboro was blessed with a gift-from-God seventy-five-degree day. I doled out sidewalk chalk to Bethie and Jay—a stocking stuffer I'd hidden so well in my mania to purchase Christmas presents early that I'd forgotten where I'd stashed it until the packing— and sat on the front stoop, face tilted blissfully to the sun.

"Watch that melanoma," Ruth called from her driveway.

"I'm soaking up vitamin D," I said without opening my eyes. "And avoiding going to the grocery store."

"Come soak and avoid over here and keep me company."

I looked. Ruth was nearly obscured by a flowering tree poking from the trunk of her car. With every heaved jerk, pale petals fluttered to the driveway. "Yoshino cherry," she said from within the branches. It took the two of us to wrestle the unwieldy trunk and root ball into a wheelbarrow. Ruth clasped the handles firmly and puffed midway into the front yard. "Plant yourself there," she said, pointing to the grass. "I'm planting the tree here." She picked up a shovel, stuck its blade into the ground, and jumped on it as though it were a pogo stick.

"Shouldn't trees be planted in the fall?" I asked.

"They *should*," Ruth agreed, "but it's taken me this long to decide between a sugar maple and a cherry." She lifted and emptied a shovelful of earth on the grass. "One is gorgeous in the spring, one's magnificent in the fall."

A convertible of joyriders whizzed past in a red-striped blur. "Slow down, idiot!" Ruth bellowed futilely at the car's disappearing taillights. "Next time you come home," she instructed me, "park your car on the street so traffic is forced to brake. I'm working on City Hall to put in a sidewalk. For strollers and trikes and chalk," she said, gesturing to our children busily defacing the Campbell front walk with their thick pastels. "But apparently the Fisher Park area is still considered too much of a 'transient neighborhood,' in euphemistic real estate jargon, to qualify. Which translates as not having enough clout, unlike the mansion-dwellers farther north, where the maids walk the dogs. On sidewalks," she added, and grunted with exertion as the sharp head of the shovel severed a root. The cleanly sliced remnant shone white as a turnip against the red Carolina clay.

"Wow," Jay said appreciatively.

"Which way to da beach?" Ruth asked him, flexing her muscle in Charles Atlas imitation. Jay giggled.

Chin to knees, I gazed out over Ruth's lawn. Her front porch view was the same as mine. Fisher Park roughly circled a sloping wooded valley of city park threaded with footpaths and a sometimes creek. Its swing set, climbing fort, and basketball court had been attractive pluses to our house purchase. The blunt square roofs of high-rise buildings downtown were visible through the interlaced, winter-naked branches of trees. Two blocks to the left and behind us, raised railroad tracks ran between high kudzu-covered banks.

"We're just a close-to-downtown has-been neighborhood touted as newly stylish. A mixture of two-career childless types, fringe strangeos, *artistes,* dying old-sters, and brave newcomers like yourself," Ruth con-tinued. She knelt, satisfied herself that the hole was sufficiently deep, and, straightening, began chopping at its bottom to loosen the dirt. "Reed and I call them"—she pointed to one house—"the Neatniks. They never miss a trash pickup day. Never leave a newspaper in the driveway. Change the flowers in the front pots on schedule. Over there," she said, "are the Nameless Nooners. Unmarrieds who come home for a lunch-hour quickie. And presumably human beings live in that Williamsburg blue number four doors down. But we've never seen anyone, so we've named them the Moles." She opened a plastic bag of peat moss and laboriously mixed its contents with the broken earth below her.

Sloan picked up a dirt clod and threw it back in the hole. "Cut that out, Sloan," Ruth said.

"I like the idea of using your maiden name for her first name."

"Well. Ultimate egomania or just good old Southern convention, depending on your point of view. Whatever gender came out was doomed to be Sloan. Same for Grayson—my maiden middle. Poor little abandoned name."

"Didn't Reed mind that no one was named for him?"

Ruth slit open the burlap root bag with a knife and regarded me mildly. "They are. They'll have his name forever: Campbell."

I couldn't argue. A car horn blared, and I turned as Ruth waved to a wood-paneled station wagon.

"Was that Roslyn Lawrence?"

"Yeah. The Mother Superior. Surely she's been over with a casserole?"

"She . . . stopped by for a minute," I responded, reluctant to admit to Ruth the circumstances under which she'd come. Unlike Ruth, Roslyn Lawrence, more wedded to manners, did knock on my door. When I opened it, she was standing there holding a grubby Jay by the hand.

"Isn't this your child?" she'd asked. I stared. "Did you know he was outside alone?"

Though the woman's tone carried helpful concern, not accusation, conflicting emotions washed over me, flushing my face and dampening my armpits. Shame, for having been so desperate to entertain Jay that I'd let him go to the park with a pack of crackers and a warning to be careful. Anger, that this stranger had taken it upon herself to amend and implicitly criticize my parenting, my authority. Fear, because I'd placed my child in jeopardy for some selfish peace. And gratitude to the woman before me for intervening. I mustered what dignity I was able. "Yes, I knew. I could see him from the window." Passing the buck, I said, "You didn't get too close to the street, did you, Jay?"

He was unfazed by my shifting of blame. "Mom. You said things got stiff when they died."

"They do." I shifted uncomfortably as Roslyn stood watching and probably disapproving that I'd obviously already discussed as difficult a subject as death with a youngster.

"I found a bird in her yard"—he pointed at Roslyn—"and it wasn't bloody or stiff. But it was dead."

At her cue, she smiled. "We haven't met. I'm Roslyn Lawrence."

"Pril Henderson. And this is Jay."

"Why, Mom?" Jay persisted, immune to adult introductions.

Roslyn pointed over her shoulder to the large

33

colonial-style house across the park. "Birds fly into the windowpanes of our second-story sleeping porch," she said apologetically. "Apparently they see their reflection, or an enemy, or something. I was in my bedroom and heard it . . ."—she faltered— "thunk, and looked outside and he was there. Your son, I mean. Alone."

"Say, Mom," Jay persisted. *Say*, he said, meaning *tell me*. "Its eyes were shut. It looked like the birdie was sleeping but it was dead. Why was the body soft, Mom?"

I knelt to Jay's level. He was my adventuresome child, born to revel and rejoice in the outdoors. Park swings and slides held no allure for him, no surprises, but the creek offered limitless possibilities of dams and frogs and quicksilver minnows. I worried about sewage and broken glass while he gleefully explored the dark cylindrical cave of the head-high drainage tunnel running beneath the road. Regeneration of earthworms amazed him; he held slugs in equally high esteem.

"I don't know, Jay," I said. "He hit the glass so hard it broke his . . . wings," I said. Jay's lower lip trembled with the injustice, the heartlessness of nature's random cruelties. "Please," I said, turning to Roslyn, "come in. It's the least thanks I can offer you for bringing Jay home."

"No, no," she'd said, backing down the steps. "I'm in the middle of meatloaf."

Now, as the car braked at the end of the street, I

glimpsed the unmistakable silhouette of a child's car seat. "And her husband is—Berk, right?" I asked. "Is that a nickname too?"

"Yeah, short for Berserk."

"Not really."

"No, not really. Short for Berkshire." Ruth grinned.

I admired the Lawrence house again, by far the largest home in Fisher Park, with formal white porch columns and floor-to-ceiling first-story windows. A massive magnolia tree towered over the front yard, a wide swath of semicircle lawn bordered by rhododendron. "Their house is beautiful," I said.

"Unlike our hovels, the grand manse has"—Ruth's voice dropped to a mock reverential whisper—"twelve-foot ceilings and hardwood floors up and down! Very BFD. Big fucking deal."

"I hardly ever see but one car there."

"Berk isn't home much. He's an accountant, but he commutes forty-five minutes back and forth to the office. And if it's hunting season somewhere, he's gone on the weekends too."

"How old is her baby?"

Ruth looked puzzled. "Baby?"

"I saw a car seat."

She laughed. "Oh, right. Her 'baby,' David, is in the seventh grade. The other two boys, William and Trey, are in ninth and twelfth. But they're away at boarding school. Berk's all-male alma mater, natch. Not that Roslyn had any say-so about their going."

"So why the car seat?"

Kelly

"Roslyn is a volunteer driver for the Children's Home." I knew of the Childen's Home, the respected statewide adoption agency headquartered in Greensboro. "With her boys nearly grown and gone, Roslyn still needs that maternal fix. She delivers newborns from the birth mother to the Home, where adopting parents pick up their new babies. I'm surprised your children haven't sniffed Roslyn out yet. She's a Pied Piper mother."

"What do you mean?"

"You know the Pied Piper mothers. The ones who are irresistible to children, draw them like a magnet. Mine love her. And why not? She dresses up as a witch at Halloween, greets them with specially wrapped treats at her door, where the teeth of her pumpkin spell out 'Happy Halloween.' She invites them over during Christmas holidays to make cookies. She buys their raffle tickets and dispenses Band-Aids and saves Campbell's Soup labels to trade for school VCRs. When Roslyn was eight months pregnant with Trey, she took his older brother William and six friends to the Coliseum to see a monster truck demonstration for his birthday party."

"My God." I thought of the limp leftover shrouds of deflated balloons—birthday remnants—that dangled from the lamppost at our old house for months. "I'm missing a birthday gene," I said.

"No shit," Ruth replied. "The definition of tedious."

"She sounds like somebody I'd hate."

36

Ruth scattered a cup of grainy fertilizer into the hole and stood up. Her response was thoughtful. "The thing is, you can't *not like* Roslyn. I think she may be the most . . . the most . . . *feminine* female I've ever met. Roslyn changes her clothes and brushes her hair before Berk gets home every night, to a full dinner. She must be the last person on the planet who serves a meat and two vegetables. I dare you. Knock on her door anytime after five P.M. and see if the Pachelbel *Canon* isn't playing. She's even got David trained to do his homework then, so Berk can have her full attention. Besides, poor David's days in Fisher Park are numbered. Prep school looms." Ruth tucked loose strands of her hair behind her ear. "Then there's me, rending my clothes and staggering to the door when Reed gets home. He claims he just pulls in the driveway and honks so that I know my shift is over."

I laughed, but Ruth didn't. "Do you know," she said with wonder, "she only uses cloth napkins. She irons his boxers." Her voice was soft. "I have actually heard Roslyn say, 'Berk likes me to wear only Chanel Number 5.' " Ruth tamped the dirt around the slender trunk. "Roslyn's harmless," she said, then again, "You can't not like Roslyn.

"Berk, though . . . ," Ruth continued, shaking her head, "Berk's a different story."

"He introduced himself to me last week at the pet store. My mother sent Jay money for a"—I grimaced—"pet as a moving present."

Ruth looked at me with a wry smile. "Yes, I heard

all about it, thanks very much. Now Grayson's pestering me for a pet. Keeping up with the Hendersons. A parakeet, right?"

I nodded. Still mourning the poor bashed bird he'd found in the Lawrences' yard, Jay had contentedly selected a green-hued parakeet, dubbing it Pete before it had even been paid for.

"What was Berk doing, buying rawhide bones for his hunting dogs?"

I was amazed by Ruth's prediction. "That's right."

"He kennels them somewhere outside the city limits."

"Do you know what he said? First he asked Jay, 'Wouldn't you rather have a dog? Every boy needs a dog.' My God, Jay's only four. Personally, I was bidding on something even simpler, a chameleon or hermit crab." Ruth laughed. "And then, he whispered in my ear, *laughing*, 'A bird for a pet? Don't blame me if he grows up to be queer.'"

Ruth stood from her crouch where she'd been spreading pine needle mulch at the base of the newly planted tree. Copper-colored needles poked comically like quills from her hair. But her words were weighted with disgust. "Once, some stranger had their dog in the park, and it darted out into the street and was run over by a car. Belly split, terrible. The owner was distraught, you can imagine, crying, struggling pathetically to pick the animal up. And Berk came outside, took a look at it, and said, 'Do you want me to shoot him?'" Ruth shook her head at the memory. "And you know what? The dog lived. Months later, she came back with him, to show us."

She brushed dirt from the knees of her jeans. "And yet Roslyn loves him. I guess there's no accounting for taste." She arched, stretching her arms wide. "Done, except for watering. And I'm already paying for it. Oh, my aching back."

"Why'd you buy such a big tree?"

She shook her head resolutely. "That's one of the reasons I opted against a sugar maple. They take too long to grow up. I'm afraid I might not be around long enough to enjoy it." She impulsively lay prone beneath it, the pine straw a stiff and scratchy pillow for her head, and squinted into the scant shade cast by the Yoshino's thin branches. "In two springs, you'll thank me."

Across the park a driving mower sputtered to life in the Lawrences' yard. Ruth lifted her head. "First time this spring," she said. "Look at that." A young woman sat astride the mower, a long blond braid hanging from beneath her baseball cap. "In my next life I'm having a yard man, correction, yard *person*, like Katrina yonder. Some Norse-looking goddess who'll fluff and puff my pine needles."

She paused dramatically in the act of gathering tools and crumpled bags. "Ssh!" she hushed, and the boys whirled guiltily away from the curb, where they'd been brazenly jumping into the street. Ruth cocked her head, listening. "Quick quick quick!" she cried. "It's coming! Grayson, get the penny jar! Hurry, guys, this way!"

Once again I did as told, snatching Bethie to my hip as Ruth did Sloan, and following her through the backyard and up the gradual hill. Jay and Grayson were at our heels, the tinny ring of pennies in the baby food jar keeping time with our panting and the bump of the girls' bottoms against our hipbones. I could hear it too, now, nearly feel its rushed approach beneath the soles of my sneakers: the train. We clambered through the brittled, wiry kudzu vines, buoyant as bedsprings, and laid six pennies on the shined-silver tracks. The train was still nowhere in sight, but the distant clanged warnings at a downtown crossing and the faint vibration of the narrow rails beneath our fingers confirmed Ruth's shouted urgings.

"Get back! Back to the street!" she called, and we did, dragging the boys by their overall straps, and laughing. In the charged heated air of the sidelines we counted the cars and chanted choo-choo caboose songs until the last flatbed rushed past and it was safe to scurry up the banks again. Between the rails and pebbles and vines we scavenged, seeking the ordinary coins transformed into perfectly flattened discs, slivers of copper whose friction-warmed smoothness we pressed to our palms and cheeks and lips all the way home. It was a good day, a lucky day. For planting trees, and penny treasures, and more.

$\mathscr{C}$ hapter 4

And would you describe your friendship, your relationship *with the defendant as 'close,' Mrs. Henderson?"*

I nodded. From her seat across the courtroom she smiled at me, the same wide, welcoming, impish smile of that comic bedroom scenario. "Through fire and flood," she'd said.

"You'll have to answer orally, Mrs. Henderson. The court reporter can't record head shaking."

"Yes."

"How close?"

"Yes. Very."

"Come, Mrs. Henderson, more than a monosyllable would be helpful and hardly incriminating."

"Objection!"

"Sustained."

The prosecutor sighed wearily. "Were you and $\mathscr{D}\!\!\bigcirc$

Ruth Campbell as close as, as intimate as, say, sisters?"
I looked at Ruth again. "No."
"No?" the prosecutor mimicked with mock stun.
He looked dramatically heavenward for patience.
"No," I repeated. "Closer."

What binds women to one another?

No one asked me this question, during all of it. No husband, attorney, or judge. Ruth and I never asked each other either. We already knew.

For ten years our families were next-door neighbors. We borrowed tools, exchanged birthday and Christmas and anniversary presents, stashed spare keys in each other's kitchens, carpooled. We had children the same ages and gender who attended the same schools and took the same piano and karate lessons and played on the same soccer and basketball teams. We spent time together as couples, grilling on weekend evenings, going to movies and concerts, taking beach and mountain and lake vacations. These are all contributing factors, but they are neither guarantees nor determinants of friendship, or intimacy, or loyalty. They don't define or explain the relationship between Ruth and me.

Or the relationship that *was*. It's been two years since she left; a year since the trial. From my daily sentry stance just inside the front door, I watch for the mailman. He's late today. So is Beth, who should by now be home from the mall, where she's trying to figure out exactly what is wrong with her clothing, and therefore her life. At thirteen, she's firmly and only Beth now, no longer Bethie. But she was still Bethie when she asked me after a devastating day of fourth grade, "Are you and Ruth best friends?" Her sworn "best friend" had dumped her because she'd found another best friend, one who had given her half a Snickers bar at lunch.

"You and Ruth seem to be joined at the hip," Roslyn had commented not long before that.

Scotty's tone, on a different occasion, was nastier. "What's the deal with you two? Do you have your periods in sync too?"

I'd bent over the laundry baskets, grinning to myself. We swapped period stories. The white jeans and sheets soaked in cold water and Clorox. The ruined underwear. Ruth's tales were always better—ghastlier and funnier, more bizarre—than mine. A bikini swimsuit bottom forever relegated to the back drawer after she'd blithely sunned her legs on the terrace, reading. Feeling with certain dread a warm dampness between her crossed legs during jury duty. "What was I supposed to do?" she'd squeaked, doubled over with laughter. "Your Honor, I require a recess to stanch my menstrual flow." Climbing out of her week-old car to discover a burgundy blotch on the pristine "tawny doe" upholstery of the driver's seat. "Do you realize the value of this vehicle has just dropped five hundred dollars?" Reed grumbled as he furiously scrubbed the stain with detergent. Dryly unfazed,

Ruth said, "Why do you think they call it 'the curse'?"

Here's what we didn't talk about: Fingernails. Manicures. Stereo components. Centerpieces and curtains and orgasms; or the lack thereof. But in a ten-year span, surely there was nothing else we didn't discuss, commiserate, or exult over.

Children, husbands, love, sex. "I made a private deal with myself," Ruth proclaimed one morning over coffee. "I'm going to have sex every time Reed initiates, morning or night, and see how long he'll last." Two weeks later, when I'd forgotten all about her sex pact, she yelled across the driveway, "Nine days! Nine straight! Uncle!"

"I read that the average sixteen-year-old male consciously or unconsciously thinks about sex every seven seconds," she said as we sat on a bench watching high school boys playing basketball in the park. "Every seven seconds! Jesus."

"Where does she get that stuff?" Scotty asked when I told him. "And who cares?" As with the period stories—"Why don't you wear an extra pad or whatever?"—Scotty failed to see the black humor, or the poignancy, or the importance of any of it. Indeed, who cared except for Ruth and me? Eventually I stopped telling him.

"Mom!" Jay had fumed when he overheard me laughing to Ruth about his fifth grade history project. He'd fashioned the title of the report entirely in staples: THE LINCOLN-DOUGLAS DEBATES spelled out in chunky metal capitals. "Why are you telling Ruth that?"

"It's not a big deal, Jay. I thought it was funny."

"What's funny about it?"

I was surprised by his vehemence over something so trivial. "I'm sorry, Jay; nothing's funny about it."

Later, Scotty too had scolded me. "It wasn't intended to hurt Jay's feelings," I protested.

"So why tell her at all?"

"Because I knew she'd love hearing it. Last week Sloan used pinking shears to cut her doll bald-headed, then threw the plastic hair outside because her teacher told her that birds make their nests with hair. Grayson calls socks that he's worn more than one day 'hard socks.'" I'd laughed. "Ruth and I always pass those kinds of details along. They make life worth living."

Scotty frowned. "Don't expect Jay to understand the subtleties of your relationship with Ruth."

Details.

Psychiatrists and theorists and essayists, and yes, feminists, dissect and analyze and assign universal themes and theories to explain what binds women: the desire to nurture, the experience of childbirth, the constant striving to succeed and excel in a male-dominated world. And surely these are our common causes. But what truly, more accurately, binds women is the incremental collective trivia of hilarities and heartbreaks, humiliation and humdrum amassed over telephones and fences, over laundry baskets and garden beds, on back stoops and park benches, in driveways and dry cleaners, in checkout lanes and carpool lines. It's the parallel details of their existence that bind and entwine women with one another: the minutiae of children and husbands and homes.

Details. Women are bound by the perpetual presence of smudges on windows and storm doors from children's hands and lips. By fending off begging dinnertime solicitations from the Handicapped Veterans of America, the Paralyzed Police Corps, the Eternal Peace people hawking cemetery plots. By dust balls the size of mice beneath beds. By T-shirts tinted pink from red socks in the washer, and permanent orange streaks on pillowcases from a melted crayon in the dryer. By pathetically comic statistics calculated at kitchen counters. "I have a theory that every individual actually has only ten meals in their culinary repertoire, and they just cook variations over and over all their lives," I said.

"Makes sense to me," Ruth said, opening a bag of bread. As they waited for their lunches, the children were mindlessly flattening potato chips into salty specks on their paper plates. "Let's see. Two sandwiches times three hundred sixty-five equals one thousand four hundred sixty slices of bread per year," she continued.

"How about peanut butter?" I asked Bethie.

"Ick," she replied. "Elephant breath."

"What else is there?" Grayson asked.

"Pimento cheese. Egg salad."

"Gross," he countered. "Goo food."

"Aren't you going to wash those first?" I asked Ruth as she cut apples into slices.

"Personally, I believe not washing fruit for my children makes them more resistant to disease." She reached into the refrigerator, pulled out a chicken, and holding its plucked and stumpy wings, walked the headless body across the cutting board. "Thirty-seven years old, and I still have to dance with a raw chicken to figure out which side is the breast." She plopped the greasy meat into a pan and shoved it in the oven. Goo food and dancing chickens and ten meals. This is what bound us.

Layman diagnoses and symptom-swapping. "Feel her," I would say to Ruth, certain that my friend's palm was more sensitive to Bethie's fevered forehead than mine. "Does his throat look red to you?" Ruth asked me, shining a Boy Scout flashlight beam into Grayson's gullet. We were bound by calamine-crusted chicken pox and nit-picking scalps side by side during a lice infestation at school. By the nagging worry of a child's coughing in the night. As mother, one should rise from warmth and slumber to dispense medicine and sympathy. At two and three in the morning I would look automatically for lights in Ruth's house, taking comfort that she too was awake and active, summoned by a needy child at a gravelike hour of darkness.

We were bound by sick days and snow days and

Saturdays—periods of sheer maintenance with no accomplishment or forward progression, waiting only for time to pass. By the availability or unavailability of baby-sitters. Jenny, who went to check on a sleeping Jay and knocked out her front teeth on the forgotten steel chin-up bar across his doorway. Alice, whom I discovered beneath her boyfriend one midnight on our brick terrace. "Dry humping?" Reed had laughed. "Ouch. Do you think she had brick burns instead of rug burns?"

We were linked by memories too, of mean girl friends and old boyfriends. With a mixture of longing and laughter, we recalled the names of those early flames with not nearly as much fondness as for the wild torrential feelings, the giddy rush of anticipation, that accompanied those usually unrequited or unresolved affairs of the heart. We didn't miss them, regret those early crushes and one-sided passions, but we wondered what had happened to those boys now men, where they were and how—or with whom— they had wound up.

We anguished and grieved over horrific accounts of accidental deaths: the daughter who suffocated on a chunk of unchewed hot dog; the son run over by an unattended golf cart. The sleeping infant in a crib eaten by the family's escaped boa constrictor; the teenager who, blood draining from every orifice, died in mere hours of a meningitis bacteria with the incurable unstoppable force of a hurtling train. Unanswerable questions or puerile games, each bound us.

"Here's what I hate," Ruth would say. "People who think out loud on the phone."

"Here's what I hate," I said. "People who drive with their dogs in their laps."

"Here's what I hate," Ruth said. "Chihuahuas."

Confessing, we shared the sick strange stunts of females in prolonged exclusive company at summer camp, boarding school, sorority houses. Of not shaving for so long that it hurt to pull on socks. Of Ruth's prep school roommate who'd fashioned a toupee of pubic hair. Of what was sexy, and what was not. "Patent leather high heels," Ruth avowed, "with no stockings."

"Bare shoulders in strapless dresses," I offered.

"Diamond studs with blue jeans," Ruth added, then caught herself. "Listen to us. Who are we making this list for? Everything on it has to do with what's sexy about women!"

We were bound by short-lived forays into extra-curricular activities and self-improvement. Bridge lessons that ended after only four sessions. "I can't do it," I said, driving home with Ruth after a late evening with six other bridge neophytes, chattering women. "Either I say something I wish I hadn't said, or I hear something I wish I hadn't heard."

"Suits me," Ruth agreed. "I'm buffaloed by no trump. Besides, I'll be my mother soon enough without rushing the process."

We joined the Y, lured as much by the promise of free baby-sitting as taut thighs. But the very atmosphere of the fitness room defeated us: the grim sterility of hissing, pumping weight and aerobic machinery combined with the equally grim expressions of panting, sweating humans. Besides, Ruth got so distracted by the wall of flickering television screens that she routinely fell off the treadmill, sending the fitness director scurrying over to make certain she hadn't had a heart attack. We returned to our walks instead.

One Mother's Day, Scotty and Reed conspired to give us identical gifts: a personal consultation with a "color expert," who came to our house, held sheets of construction paper beside our faces, and gravely decided which tints and hues were most flattering to our complexions. For months we each dutifully carried a keychain of tiny color chips, like paint or formica samples, in our purses to help us choose the correct shades when we shopped for clothes. Years later I found the color ring stuffed far at the back of my underwear drawer, among crumpled slips of paper that had long since lost their scent—perfume samples enclosed with store bills that Ruth and I used as cheap sachets. I tied the loop of chips to the bow of Ruth's fortieth-birthday present. "I can hardly remember that phase of my life," I said, shaking my head. "Can you believe we were ever that superficial?"

"No, Pril," she insisted, and corrected me. "We were *never* superficial." She fingered the bright wrapping and matching gold-flecked ribbon, an expensive splurge on gift wrap. "You used your good stuff," she said, and opened the coordinated enclosure card. I laughed at how our minds worked so in tandem. *"Happy Birthday,"* I'd written. *"I love you so much I used one of my gift tags."*

I return to the door, rechecking as though some missive might be hiding in the narrow brass mail slot. Waiting and watching.

At the grand manse across the park, snaking, menacing tentacles of kudzu have stealthily begun to overtake the shrubbery once meticulously pruned. Blighted by public history, the Lawrence house hasn't sold. The Campbells', blighted only by small personal history, has.

The owners-to-be next door have erected a privacy fence, stretching to the street and more definitely delineating and separating our yards. I was standing beside the new fence, glossy white with fresh paint, when Scotty came home from work last night. He clasped my neck with his free hand in an uncharacteristic gesture of affection. "It's all right, Pril. Good fences make good neighbors, right?"

I nodded silently, resigned to another change. He rubbed his scratchy cheek against my forehead, and with a sudden rush of old love—that early, uncompromised, uncomplicated love—I hugged him too.

The hulking behemoths of earth-moving machinery next door are temporarily tamed, quiet and parked at dangerous-looking angles near the edge of the yard like stranded relics. Somewhere beneath the packed and treaded red clay being graded into submission lies the sidewalk that Ruth, our self-appointed speed and sidewalk vigilante, fought so fiercely for. It came too late, though, and I think of the two of us, jogging behind wobbling two-wheelers on the basketball court in the park, clutching our children's shirt collars and panting as we dodged the diminutive bombs of prickly sweet-gum balls. Memoraic details.

I glimpse Ruth's Yoshino cherry tree, or what is left of it. It will surely die, so severely have the new owners pruned it in hopes it will survive the mutilation and grading of the yard. Remarkable, how what we do to people, living things, in order to assure their survival often kills them.

Ruth had been right in her predictions; like our children and incomes, the cherry tree had grown, flourished. With every successive spring it widened into a lace parasol of palest pink above our heads, and we picnicked beneath the blossom-laden branches, frothy as a milkshake. Even after the children dismissed and scorned the seasonal ritual, Ruth and I sentimentally maintained it. We'd lie down and gaze upward, waiting for the faintest breeze to send a silent shower of petals falling like snowflakes on our faces.

According to the morning news, it's snowing today in Idaho. By the calendar spring is officially here, the same month she left. I'll miss the Yoshino this year, as I do Ruth every day.

Details: minor, ludicrous, banal to the bone. From

the superficial to the substanceless to the sublime, all were important, none less or more worthy in defining and cementing and sustaining our friendship.

Yet. But. When I think of all the aspects that bound the two of us, I see now that I failed to consider the answer to another question the experts ask each other, the clichéd, more-famous query: What do women want?

Chapter 5

"All right," Ruth said to me at the bus stop the radiantly golden morning after Labor Day. "No more excuses. Get thee inside and create."

We grinned at each other idiotically. Bethie and Sloan were entering first grade, and the anticipated unadulterated solitude of their eight-hour weekday absence held as much prized promise as a month of Christmas Days to a child.

I think of Ruth two time zones away, with her morning still before her, inviolate. She knew I wanted to write, knew of my strange strong need to record, describe, explain.

People experience swift stabs of mortality, chimeras of death, at funerals or in accidents and illnesses, even in the changing faces of their growing children. But for me, mortality comes not as whiff or whisper, but as a bold stinging slap, in bookstores.

54

When I was a child, the rows of C. S. Lewis, Laura Ingalls Wilder, Frances Hodgson Burnett on a bookstore shelf, even stacked yellow spines of Nancy Drew mysteries, made me tremble with greed. Now the aligned and glossy volumes with enigmatic titles both lure me to read and taunt me to write. Yearning evolves into near panic. With my time my own, I wanted to write. To tell and narrate. "Are you writing?" Ruth would ask whenever she called. "Typing," I would answer, fearful of offending the muse, and not allowing myself the unearned legitimacy of the title "writer."

Ruth returned to the passion of her childhood: horses. Each morning as I sat down before the glaring electric eye of my word processor, I would see her out the window preparing to leave for Pearson's Stables twenty miles away. She still easily wore the dove-gray second-skin jodhpurs with high black boots I'd admired at Kiahwassee.

"Let me read something," she said two months later as we sat in the park. Leaves drifted lazily down, harbingers of winter. Ruth understood my drive to write better than I appreciated her need to ride, and would relate to me phrases, incidents, or details she thought useful, interesting, or poignant.

I ran my finger over names carved in the wooden bench and thought of the scant scribbled entries in my notebook, where the margins were marred with similar graffiti, doodles of spiders, spectacled eyeballs. "There's nothing worth reading yet."

"Oh bull, surely there's something. Jesus, don't 'journal.' I hate when people talk about 'journaling.' "

I shook my head. "Whatever I write seems paltry. Nothing tragic or significant has ever happened to me. Nothing with merit. No great . . . moral battle."

"Please. The day-to-day battle is the most moral, tragic, and heroic battle anyone fights. Everything's a story. Write about this. About us."

I smiled.

"What?" she asked.

"I remember getting out of college, wondering what on earth I was going to 'do for a living.' I became so desperate to latch onto something that I began looking at literally *anything* as possible employment: fire hydrants, pencils, stoplights. Someone had to build them, sell them, advertise them. All those jobs. Like your saying 'everything's a story.' " I crunched crisp withered leaves beneath my feet for emphasis. "But I don't want to write slice-of-life stories."

"Fine then, go ahead," Ruth said. "Pander to the masses. Prostitute yourself. Write a happy-ending romance."

"In my opinion and vast experience," Ruth observed, "either you pick your passions or they pick you."

She had chosen to ride, but perhaps the feminism chose her. I can tick them off, those early incidents

and indications; some slight, some comic. Shunning
the "patriarchal structure" of the church. Active disdain for Berk Lawrence's manner, rather than simply
discounting or ignoring it. Her delight in discovering
that Sloan had penned a coat and tie on her picture in
the elementary school yearbook; her indignation with
Grayson's claim that boys were obviously smarter
than girls since more men than women appeared on
the *Jeopardy!* television game show. On a trip to the
mall she'd returned from the rest room noticeably irritated.

"Have you seen these 'Infancy Centers' in ladies'
rooms now, with fold-down changing tables, and little stools with seat belts in the stalls so mothers can
park their babies and pee? I've a good mind to check
out the men's room and see if they include the same
handy amenities for males. What, they don't assume
men bring their children to the mall?"

I dipped my warm pretzel in mustard and chewed
off a gummy bite of dough. "Who cares? I'm just
grateful not to be lugging diaper bags anymore."

"*I* care. It's sexist."

But she'd only laughed when I showed her the
book I ordered from News and Novels. "Don't you
know the images in this book are degrading and hu-
miliating to women?" the clerk had demanded from
her authoritative position behind the raised counter
as she handed it over to me. Titled *Women, Heroes
and a Frog*, the book was a slender paperbound collection of quotes and black-and-white photographs.

"Look at this," the clerk had continued, without waiting for my response. She found a page and pushed it in my face, reading: " ' "*The desire of a man for a woman is not directed at her because she is a human being, but because she is a woman. That she is a human being is of no concern to him.*" *Immanuel Kant.*' Or this: ' "*Girls we love for what they are; young men for what they promise to be.*" *Johann Wolfgang von Goethe.*' How can you buy such a book?"

"I like quotes," I'd feebly defended. "I'm a writer."

She peered over her tortoiseshell glasses as I fumbled for correct change. "A writer? Should I know you?" she asked. Cowed and confronted, I slunk out with my purchase. She hadn't offered me a bag.

"Oh well," Ruth had said. "They're dead white men. This one's okay: ' "*When you educate a man you educate an individual, when you educate a woman you educate a whole family.*" *Charles McIver.*' Whoever he was." She sorted through the mail she'd brought with her, flyers, magazines, bills. "It's not as bad as, say, *this,*" she said, showing me an ad for St. Pauli Girl beer. "*You never forget your first girl,*" the slogan claimed. " 'You never forget your first girl,' " Ruth read aloud with scorn. "How catchy. How cleverly double-entendred. What those Madison Avenue suits mean is, you never forget the first girl you screwed."

As usual, a half-dozen catalogs, colorful and enticing, had come to both of us. "These catalogs make

me want things I never knew I needed until the mail
came," Ruth said. "There," she said, pointing.
"That's what I want for my next birthday." An impossibly healthy, impossibly blond woman was riding
a horse through a grassy sunlit field of flowers. In the
background, scenic snow-capped mountains jutted
into a cloudless, azure sky.

"The coat?" I asked, pointing to the turquoise-
studded, furred, and sueded coat the woman was
wearing. "Looks more like nauga-rabbit than mink. I
know; the horse?"

"The setting." Ruth checked the catalog title.
" 'Sundance Country.' Look at those mountains. The
wildflowers. Wonder where the picture was taken?"

I shrugged. "One of those square states out West. I
can never remember."

Ruth wasn't militant or maniacal on the subject of
feminism. She was more interested in the intellectual
aspects of the cause than social ills or specific injus-
tices of unequal pay, maternity leave, derelict fathers.
She read aloud to me from feminist-oriented essays
and articles, nonfiction works with six-word titles,
the occasional biography of Virginia Woolf or Vita
Sackville-West. I indulged her, or else didn't pay much
attention. Ruth read for education and reality; I read
for invention and escape.

Occasionally, though, her convictions erupted, as
they did one Saturday night when we gathered for an
impromptu dinner at our house. "Allow me to turn

my kitchen over to you," I said to Reed. Berk and Roslyn Lawrence were on their way.

"*Merci,*" Reed answered. Ruth spoke admiringly of Reed's strong feminine streak. He was a fabulous cook, and when the Campbells entertained it was Reed who arranged flowers, chose the wine, and largely prepared the meal. "Here I am," he said good-naturedly, "your average dominated eunuch." He was painstakingly slicing zucchini and scallions into julienned matchsticks, a task made more difficult by a Velcro-and-spandex support strap he was wearing on his wrist to immobilize a Little League coaching sprain.

"What's the entree?" I asked.

"Venison."

"Berk's venison?" Berk had become an avid bow-hunter. For months he'd spent every weekend two hours out of town painstakingly constructing a tree stand and establishing a salt lick to woo deer.

"Roslyn's venison," Ruth corrected.

"Roslyn?" I asked with incredulity.

Ruth nodded. "She's gone up a tree too." I frowned, trying to graft the image of Roslyn straddling a branch, a gun muzzle to her cheek.

Ruth poured herself a glass of wine. "It must be a turn-on, is all I can figure." Reed glanced reprovingly at his wife. "Well?" Ruth demanded. "Why else would you sit in a tree all day, knock your shoulder out of whack with a shotgun, and then slit Bambi, gut to butt? There has to be a reward somewhere."

Berk and Roslyn walked through the back door, dodging a column of newspapers waiting to be recycled. "Sorry we're late," Berk apologized. "Just got off the phone with William." William, the Lawrences' eldest son, was attending the state university. "He called us to warn us about two Fs he's getting this grading period." Berk shook his head grimly. "Wonder how he'd like earning his own living instead of skipping class to party."

"I'll bring you the book I'm reading," Ruth offered. "It's called *Men Are Not Cost-Effective*." Berk looked at Ruth as though he couldn't decide whether she was serious or not, and said, "I don't read self-help manuals." He reached to shake Reed's hand and noticed the bandaged wrist. "What happened, Reed? Ruth twist your arm and break it?"

We laughed. Not Ruth. "Hilarious," she said. "If someone asked that of a woman it wouldn't be so funny."

Berk touched Ruth's arm with his index finger and drew it quickly back, shaking and blowing on it. "Ouch. Struck a nerve. I see Ruth's belligerence meter is on High tonight." He turned to me. "How's Pril, the bard of suburbia? Anything published yet?"

"Watch it," Scotty put in. "She's taking down every word you say."

"No," I said, hating Berk's question, however guileless, but grateful nevertheless that he hadn't opened with his standard conversational query, asking whether I'd read some best-selling thriller he was enamored of. I never had.

"Pay no attention to Ruth," Reed said. "She's fresh from her Ariadne group."

"Ariadne group?" I asked. "What's that?"

Ruth turned the cork over in her hand. "Five women who get together twice a month to discuss issues, books we're reading." My expression must have betrayed my surprise and hurt; it was the first I'd heard of Ruth's "group." "I don't think you'd know anyone," she said. "Martha Burnett, Fran Sykes?" I shook my head. I didn't even know the names. "Someone I struck up a conversation with in line at Best Bagels," Ruth continued, "and oh, you know Naomi." Naomi was Ruth's trainer at Pearson's. I stood by, silently justifying why I couldn't have known of the Ariadne gathering. Why Ruth might not have included me. Because she'd had her "aura" read by a massage therapist twice, and I'd expressed no small skepticism at the concept of an individual's problems being evident in their muscle tone? It wasn't a great reason, but it would have to do. "Want some wine, Roslyn?" Ruth asked.

"No," Roslyn said. "I gave up alcohol for Lent."

"I forgot," Ruth said. She poured a glass for Scotty and handed it to him. "What'd you give up, Scotty? Your subscription to *Ms.* magazine?"

"When did you get to be so sassy and brassy?" Scotty returned affectionately.

Ruth threw her arm around his neck and kissed

him on the cheek. "I've always been sassy and brassy, Scotty," she said. "I'm just sassy and brassy about something different now."

"Where are the children?" Roslyn asked. "I wanted to see them."

"Stashed at my house with pizzas and videos," Ruth said. "They came over to see you this afternoon, but you weren't there."

"I was checking on Milly Cooke. She had her tubes tied yesterday and is still too sore to do much for herself."

"I've got to do something about that myself," I said. "I keep postponing it."

"Why doesn't Scotty 'do something about that'?" Ruth said.

"Are you kidding? Scotty thinks a vasectomy will make hair grow on his palms or his voice squeak."

"Now, wait a minute," Scotty said. "No one's coming near me with a knife, but I offered to take the responsibility for birth control."

"Swell," I said dryly. "I don't know what's worse. Coitus interruptus or smelling like a tire factory."

"It costs seven times, seven times!" Ruth exclaimed, "for a woman to have her tubes tied than it does for a man to have a clip job."

"Insurance pays for it," Scotty answered. I'd seen it on our policy. "Voluntary sterilization" it was genteelly, clinically termed.

"Besides," Ruth added, "vasectomies are reversible."

Retreating from argument, Scotty took a deep swallow of his wine. In the awkward silence Berk took a flyer from his back pocket and handed it to me. "Brought you something, Pril." It was a leaflet advertising Outward Bound, the organization that leads grueling expeditions in which participants voluntarily pit themselves against nature to challenge their self-sufficiency and personal determination. "I've been put on the board," Berk said. "It's great. At the black-tie annual dinner meeting everyone wears tennis shoes with their tux."

"Congratulations," I said.

"One of the perks is giving away one free session a year, and I think you're the perfect candidate, Pril. Here, look, you have a choice between three different trips and times of year."

I studied the blurry pictures of ragged-looking Outward Bound graduates, whose enthusiastic endorsements of the program were recorded below with multiple exclamation points. After the Ariadne exclusion I was flattered by Berk's offer, but only momentarily. I handed back the brochure. "Like a loss-leader? No thanks."

Berk was astonished. "Are you kidding? This is a fantastic privilege. And opportunity. Great material for a book. Out there alone you have to do some real self-examination."

"How about me?" Ruth said.

Berk grinned. "I think you know yourself pretty well already, Ruth. This offer is strictly for Pril."

"Well, I don't blame her for declining," Roslyn put in. "Why would anyone choose to live on an open boat with four men and no bathroom for six days?"

With time and wine the evening didn't improve. Reed related a story about a new recruit in his firm who'd been wooed with a long alcohol-soaked dinner at the City Club. At midnight the raucous group had driven to Mirage, a euphemistically named "Gentleman's Club." Laughing, Reed described the gyrating, topless, G-stringed dancers. "Anything you want starts at twenty dollars, even the drinks. But the most expensive option is the showers."

"Showers?" I interrupted. "What do you mean?"

"Just what I said. Women lathering up in spotlit Plexiglas shower stalls before an audience."

Arrested by the vivid image, I realized Ruth had been silent as we laughed, dangerously silent. I turned to her. "Did you know they were going?"

Evidently it wasn't the first time the evening had been discussed. "Not until another wife mentioned it to me. Afterward," she said. "Apparently Reed had no intention of telling me."

"It was a spur-of-the-minute thing, Ruth," Reed defended himself.

"What does that have to do with not telling me? With my finding out after the fact?"

"Oh, Ruth," Berk wheedled. "Boys will be boys."

"Shut up, Berk. Don't patronize me," Ruth said. She put down her fork and turned on Reed. Her hand chopped the air. "It's not that you *went*, Reed. You've totally missed the point. It's that you didn't *tell* me. You don't *'forget'* to mention something like that." Her mouth narrowed and tightened. "You know, Reed," she said quietly, "I don't expect you to mirror my morals, but I do expect you to share your dark side with me."

In the thick ensuing silence Roslyn spoke. "Pril, Berk has a great gadget that will compress and bind those papers when you're ready to take them to the recycling center." She pointed to the stack of newspapers and smiled brightly, as if she had conveniently solved the brewing dispute. We looked down at our empty plates.

"Hey," Ruth said slyly. "I brought dessert. Everybody stay seated. It's a surprise."

She closed the swinging door to the dining room, and we fell easily back into conversation about Easter plans. Roslyn wanted to have an egg hunt for our children and their friends on her lawn. Suddenly the door reopened, and Ruth stepped dramatically from the brightly lit kitchen into the darkened dining room. But no one noticed the magnificent shortcake she carried, mounded with red berries. Ruth was naked to her waist, her breasts dollopped with whipped cream, white peaks of foam covering her nipples. "See, Reed?" she chirped, shaking her beautiful head and jiggling her cream-covered bosoms. She set the shortcake before her husband. "You can stay home and get it for free!" she whooped, and fled for the bathroom. Reed had clapped the longest and laughed the hardest.

"Maybe I'll take Berk up on his Outward Bound offer," I said as Scotty and I cleaned up after everyone had departed. "What do you think?"

"What I think is that you don't need some artificial 'test' to figure out who you are," Scotty answered mildly, but with his offhand statement some small resentment smoldered within me. "What's with Ruth spitting nails about the girlie joint? The 'I am woman, hear me roar' crack about men being cost-effective, and *Ms.* I know she's a feminist, but when did she become a rabid man-hater?"

"It's men are *not* cost-effective," I corrected archly, "and she's not 'rabid.' Ruth doesn't initiate fights, or lecture. She pokes fun at attitudes, and she's just as quick to poke fun at herself."

"The proverbial velvet hammer," Scotty said. "Why can't she just be an environmentalist or vegetarian instead?"

"And this is the proverbial 'withering look,' " I replied, fixing him with a disdainful stare. I carefully rinsed a thin-stemmed wineglass and asked, "How about that topless dessert stunt? What would you do if I did that?"

"I'd kill you," he said succinctly, then casually added, "Don't you think you spend an inordinate amount of time with Ruth?"

My mouth dented with stubbornness. "Define 'in-ordinate.' "

"I think Ruth is intentionally perverse. She looks for controversy."

"She isn't and she doesn't. She believes it."

"And just what is *it*? Does she try to convert you?"

"*Convert* me?" The smolder ignited, white-hot and fierce. I stopped Scotty as he shut and locked the dishwasher. "And suppose she is? Don't you give me enough credit, or intelligence, or *freedom* to decide and think what I want?" I switched on the disposal, taking pleasure in the churning, choking grind.

"Don't turn on the disposal when the dishwasher is running," Scotty said.

"Since the kitchen is my domain, why don't you let me run things the way I see fit?" I snapped.

"Fine," he answered, and strode from the room.

It was the first argument we'd ever had about Ruth, though it wasn't to be the last. Our infrequent scraps normally concerned petty and typical domestic conflicts: money, discipline, schedule clashes. Then there were volatile subjects, the tiptoe topics we had learned not to discuss, purposely avoided, but perhaps feminism was at the root of those disputes also.

"I hardly buy anything," Scotty said when I complained of not being consulted about the large sum he was giving to a pet charity, "I'll give away what I want."

"Of course you don't buy anything!" I shot back. "Anytime you want to go to the grocery store or buy the children's clothing I'll be glad to give you the list!"

Early in our marriage he'd told me of a married colleague's blatant one-night stand on a business trip. I'd been astonished and outraged that Scotty hadn't tried to stop him or threatened him with exposure. "You become a party to it, don't you see?" I'd asked, incensed. "You're guilty too, linked by the knowledge!" Scotty was unwavering. "All you need to know is that I'm not part of Alan's shenanigans," he said. "Forget it. I wish I'd never told you. From here on out I just won't tell you anything else about these trips." The subject had remained a scabbed sore.

"I get tired of being the heavy," I said to Scotty one weeknight after he had delighted the children with an impromptu trip for ice-cream sundaes. "I'm the one who has to settle the squabbles, mete the justice and chores, make them do their homework, and you breeze in here like Disneyland Dad."

"You could have suggested ice cream," Scotty said. "Besides, it's your job."

I threw a sponge against the counter, irritated with his complacency. "Show me where it says 'toeing the wifely line' on my job description!"

"What's in your mail?" Ruth asked that afternoon in the park, closing the Sundance catalog.

"This," I said glumly, holding out a short story rejection letter.

"So you *have* written something!" She read aloud

the editor's two-word comment: " 'Not convincing.' What's the story about?"

"A couple deciding to get divorced."

She handed it back to me and crossed her arms over her chest. "Maybe you and Scotty should separate so you can write with the voice of authority."

I crumpled the rejection letter. "You're no help."

"Okay," Ruth said. "I read an author who claimed writers need three things: silence, cunning, and exile. I'd add something else to the short list: ruthlessness. Writers need to be ruthless."

"Thanks for the advice," I said petulantly. "I'll dedicate my first book to you."

"Oh, no. You should dedicate it to Scotty."

I was surprised at her choice. "Scotty? Why Scotty? He's never read a single word I've written."

"Because he gives you the time. He lets you do what you want to do. I know," she said, "so does Reed. We're both lucky."

"That's an unusual perspective coming from an ardent feminist."

Ruth shook her head. "Loving Reed and supporting the feminist cause aren't mutually exclusive."

I regarded my friend, remembering something Roslyn had said when I related how Scotty had taken exception to Ruth's antagonistic, aggressive feminist stance that night at dinner. I had wondered aloud why Reed never seemed irritated or vexed with Ruth. "Oh no," Roslyn had said, "Reed adores Ruth. Can't you tell?" The bold simplicity of the statement had stunned me, and I had analyzed it, enviously dissecting its implications. *"Oh no. He adores her."*

"Guess where Roslyn is this afternoon," Ruth said. "Berk has clients here from Mexico and she's taking their wives to Toys 'R' Us for shopping. Being the good corporate wife."

I shook my head, amazed. "Does Roslyn ever bug you?"

" 'Bug me' how?"

"The way she is. Too good. Sickly sweet."

Ruth laughed. "This from someone who needs a weekly hit from *The Sound of Music*." She chuckled again, then paused. "Why, do you wish you were more like Roslyn?"

"Of course not! What a question."

"An analyst came to speak to my group, and said something really interesting. She suggested that often what we dislike in other people are the very traits we dislike in ourselves."

"Did you learn about 'dark sides' in your group too?"

If Ruth heard the derision in my tone, she ignored it. "Yes. A dark side is where people hide all the things they don't reveal to anyone else. The little nasties and paranoias and deficiences. Everybody has a dark side. Even Roslyn."

"I don't think I'd like to be part of your group," I said mulishly, as if I'd been asked to join.

"Oh, Pril," Ruth chuckled, "you already are."

Below us, high school boys had gathered on the

basketball court as they did every afternoon for a pickup game. They knotted their shoelaces and shed their shirts, moving as disjointedly and easily as paper-clip figures: fluid in motion but firm in their skeletons. As the game began, I marveled, as always, how no one spoke. No rules were laid down, no teams assigned, no plays discussed. They simply played, those boys, the complicated rules and rituals and strategies of the game I found incomprehensible understood or intuited between them.

"They never set rules between themselves," I said. "Never."

Ruth rolled the catalog tightly into a baton and, with a slow *plick plick plick*, dragged one fingernail down each page edge. Her eyes never left the court. "No. The rules don't change. They're already set."

We watched the graceful gliding ballet of their play, listened to the rhythmic *wap wap wap* of the dribbled ball, the hollow thudding of the backboard, the metallic clinking of the chain net as the ball passed through. We watched their bare backs and narrow hips, the sinewy stretching legs, all lanky, careless suppleness. Erotically agile, they were lovely, those boys, completely unaware of our presence or anyone's: separate yet contained, impenetrable, available only unto themselves.

"They're something, aren't they?" Ruth said softly, huskily.

I didn't need to agree; I knew what she meant. "But where are all the girls?" I finally said, musing aloud.

"You'd think they'd be here on the sidelines, hanging around. Watching and waiting."

"You know where the girls are, Pril. You've forgotten how it was," Ruth said, gazing fixedly at the scene before us. "The girls spend their afternoons driving around in cars, looking; looking everywhere for those boys who are right down there." I heard a melancholy wistfulness in her voice, not judgment. A regret for the unalterable. "The boys who'll accept them and marry them and eventually exclude them again."

$\mathscr{C}$hapter 6

Writers are hostages to mailmen. Those uniformed civil servants have no inkling of their power, how each daily delivery carries the possibility of exultation, or despair. Even Sundays and holidays sustain hope. Perhaps the following day some good word will arrive.

For two and a half years I wrote, submitted, waited, collected rejection forms, wrote, and waited. And then, on an unseasonably hot late May afternoon, with summer vacation looming long, blank, and unproductive, it finally arrived: A story had been accepted by a literary magazine across the continent, in Oregon. I read and reread the spare, precious four lines with no less thrill than if I'd been awarded the Pulitzer Prize. My first thought was of Ruth, of sharing the long-awaited triumph with her. She had taken Bethie and Sloan to the stables with her directly after school.

"Jay!" I called. "I'm going out to Pearson's to find Ruth!"

"What about soccer practice? Who'll take me?"

"I'll be back," I promised on my way out the door.

Giddy with elation, I covered the miles to the country too quickly, recklessly, until the unobtrusive sign for Pearson's Stables appeared, a wooden square dangling by rusty chains. I turned onto the rutted dirt road that wound through a half mile of forested acreage and forded the shallow rocky stream that lay in the road's path just before the paddock clearings. The creek had always delighted the children, that it was necessary to slosh through running water to reach the open fields. Bethie and Sloan were finishing third grade. They loved visiting the stables, and begged to accompany Ruth on her infrequent after-school trips. Besides playing in the stream and fields, besides the carrot chunks they bravely held on flattened palms to whiskery muzzles, they liked the stocky young woman, Naomi Pearson, who owned the stables and taught Ruth, and kept horehound candy in a jar on her desk.

"Isn't there a point where you don't take lessons anymore?" I'd asked Ruth. "If you can ride and jump and show, what's left except practice?"

"You always need more instruction," Ruth said. "Naomi is the best trainer around."

Though Ruth spoke admiringly of Naomi's knowledge and abilities, I didn't really know Naomi. Something about her inspired a slight misgiving in me;

perhaps it was simply that we had so little in common. She rarely came into town, and lived near the barn in a permanently parked mobile home whose compact accoutrements fascinated the children as well. The lure of outdoor exploring and roaming freedom— even the cozy confines of the trailer—I understood those appeals and was glad the girls had access to them. The sight of Ruth astride a galloping horse was breathtaking: the fluid grace, the movements of her body united in motion with the animal's. But with some residual summer camp fear, I never understood the attraction of horses or riding.

The one instance when Ruth had persuaded me to come riding with her, I'd picked a stupid-looking Shetland who made no effort to resist as Naomi saddled him. But I'd underestimated the pony's dimwitted demeanor. Ignoring my gruff commands and digging heels and tugging on the reins, he'd calmly plodded into a nearby orchard and, beneath the low scaly branches of an apple tree, knocked me neatly, purposely, off the saddle and into the pulpy mush of fallen fruit. Scratched, sticky, and humiliated, I gave up on the third attempt, refusing Ruth's laughed protests to try another horse. Naomi had laughed too, but I heard a tenderfoot ridicule lacing her cackle.

"HAVE YOU HUGGED YOUR HORSE TODAY?" the bumper sticker on Ruth's car fender read. How can anyone love a horse? How do you hug and nestle and nuzzle an immense and powerful beast that can maim and kill on whim? An animal smart enough to smell

fear and act upon it, with kicking hooves like can-
nonballs and great bared teeth the length and color of
old piano keys? I do not understand the complicated
language of saddles and snaffles and halters, belts and
bits and straps, withers and haunches and forelocks.
It's only the aromas of horses I appreciate, the good
musty scents of dry hay and barn lumber, the leather
of tack, a warm and rich, nearly human smell.

Beyond the creek the road cut a narrow path between wide meadows, which stretched to a fringe of
dark evergreens in the distance. Bordered by white
fences, the view was strikingly, classically pastoral.
Alone in the sun or clumped beneath the shade of ancient oaks, two dozen horses cropped grass, their long
necks gracefully arched, their tails swishing languidly
at pesky flies. The animals were serenely unaware of
my car or the clouds of dust the tires raised. I drove
on, expecting to find Ruth and the girls in one of the
three rings nearer the barn. But except for the gradu-
ated jumps of horizontal poles and hoof-bruised
shrubbery in the center, the rings were empty.

I pulled onto the packed dirt of the makeshift parking lot between Ruth's station wagon and Naomi's
roofless red jeep, faded to flesh after years of sun-
baked summers. Naomi's stifling office, the walls and
shelves cluttered with ribbons and trophies, was
empty too. Adjacent to her office was the stable itself,
and I wandered into the barn's dim dust-moted corri-
dor, the gated stalls vacant with the animals out to
pasture.

"Ruth?" I called, "Bethie? Sloan?" and finally, "Naomi?" Hearing noises at the opposite end, I turned and retraced my steps, reading the name plaques beside each stall, lettering crudely drilled and charred with a wood-burning tool. *An evening's entertainment for Naomi, no doubt,* I thought meanly.

At the end of the stable the sudden glare of the open sliding door temporarily blinded me. What I saw within the small fenced enclosure paralyzed me.

A honey-colored mare stood immobilized in the center of the ring. Literally. Lead reins had been snapped tautly to opposing fence posts, allowing no movement of her head though her great eyes darted, the yellowy whites exposed. She nervously tongued an unusual metal bit of toothed spikes that gouged the tender flesh of her lips. Handcufflike shackles at either end of an iron bar were fastened to the mare's rear ankles, forcing her hind legs into an unnatural, splayed position. Her tail had been crammed and bound in a small pathetic pouch high on her rump. Rigid and stripped, the creature whinnied piteously.

Carrying a rag-wrapped poker prod, Ruth walked into view and carelessly swabbed the mare's rump. "Okay!" she hollered. "She smells irresistible now! Bring him on!"

"Stay up near her head now, out of the way," a woman called warningly. Naomi's voice. "This fellow's revved and dangerous." From an unseen corner of the ring Naomi paced backward with short halting steps, leading another horse with obvious difficulty and caution.

The stallion was enormous. Prancing, twitching, its ears alternately alert then dangerously flattened to his head, he pawed and snorted and strained as Naomi circled him near the manacled mare.

As his hooves raised plumes of dust, his huge penis appeared, dropping from beneath the muscled body. The dangling fleshy hose was thick as a wrist, raw and pink and swollen. As I watched, speechless with the spectacle unfolding before me, the stallion reared up and forward over the mare's spread haunches, its bony knees raking her quivering flanks. Again he jumped, heavily and clumsily, over the captive mare.

And then I saw them, our pigtailed, T-shirted daughters. Their thin arms and legs were wrapped tightly around the splintery split rail fence, their eyes fixed wide with comprehension, their mouths agape with terror.

"Ruth!" I called, finding my voice. "Ruth! Don't!"

But my plea went unheard, drowned out by the metallic thudding of hooves against earth and flesh, by the frenzied grunts and snorts of the maddened stallion, feverish, frightening noises amplified in the charged and humid air. A final time the beast leaped and lunged, thrusting his rippling sweat-sheened body upon and onto the mare's shackled submissive frame. She seemed to shrink, cowed and dominated beneath his heaving, slamming straddle. My own knees shook, threatening to buckle, and my mouth filled with a sudden hot spurt of mucousy saliva at the sight of that brutal, bestial assault.

"Maybe that'll get us a state champion!" Naomi called from beside the locked and coupled animals. Oblivious of the children, she chucked Ruth on the shoulder. Then, in a horrific mime, she neighed and pawed Ruth's back.

Seething with distilled and dangerous rage, I trembled in the wide doorway, fists clenched. "Ruth!"

Ruth looked around, caught sight of me. "Pril!" she called happily, unsuspecting. Checking that Naomi had the horses, the quaking mare, the spent stallion, under control, she strode over to me. "How about that?" she said, grinning with enthusiasm. "Ever watch a breeding before? Something to see, eh?" I opened my mouth to speak but she hadn't finished. "That'll make a feminist out of you, won't it?"

"*How dare you,* goddamn you. How *dare* you?" I grabbed her upper arm, tight and hard and painfully. I fought for control, my voice graveled with threat, and pulled her back into the shadowed barn, away from our children's eyes. "With Bethie and Sloan over there not ten feet away from that scene?"

Ruth looked first at my clutching fingers and then into my eyes. "Take it easy, Pril," she said mildly. "They were perfectly safe."

"*Safe?*" I parroted hoarsely, with soft, vicious menace. "Safe from what? The horses, or you? How could you let my child be witness to that? That mute ramrodded mare, and that rutting, strutting stud. She's

80

eight years old, Ruth, *eight years old!* Do you think those children will ever forget that? Do you? Are you *happy* with the unforgettable impression you've just given them?"

"For God's sakes, Pril. They're just horses." She loosened my hand. "Since when did you become such a prude? It's just breeding, not intercourse."

"Yes, and they're just children. Jesus!" I nearly shouted, panting and damp with perspiration and fury. "And that charming little concluding episode between you and Naomi! Thank you so much for the explicit differentiation, but hereafter I'll thank you to let me handle my child's sex education. I think—I *know!*—I can show her a gentler side."

I turned and walked stonily toward the hot sunlit enclosure, forming some inadequate explanation for Bethie. Behind me, Ruth spoke. "I didn't intend for it to shock them, Pril." I kept walking. She chuckled. "Look at it as a lesson in feminism! Maybe you can use it in a story!"

I pivoted and covered the space between us in three steps. "How very fortunate," I hissed inches from her face in icy, enunciated syllables. "How very *convenient* that Reed goes to work all day and brings home a paycheck so you can stay home and be a feminist!"

Though her lips and eyes narrowed under the vitriolic assault, I wasn't finished, and gave her a cursory, childish shove. The forgotten acceptance letter I still clutched dropped in a small crumpled wad to the fine silt of the barn floor. Ruth leaned over and picked it up. She unfolded it, read it, and raised her eyes to mine.

"Congratulations," she said calmly, but her tone was tinged with sarcasm. "At long last. That's just wonderful, Pril. Everything is just perfect for you now, isn't it? Perfect, perfect, perfect. Perfect home, perfect family, and now perfect story."

"Mommy?"

I turned. Bethie's small silhouette was framed in the unremitting glare of the doorway. She hesitated, and the thin voice, the frailty of her shadowed body brought unbidden tears to my eyes. "I'm hungry," she said. "Can we go home?"

I looked once more at Ruth. "You bet, Bethie," I said, my eyes never leaving Ruth's. "You bet."

"Sloan wants to come too."

"Fine," I said, and protectively grasped her shoulders. "Let's go."

Either unable or unwilling to articulate them, or sensing my own distress, the girls asked no questions on the endless trip back. Once home they scampered to play school upstairs, where I heard the occasional stern command to their dolls to behave. Resourceful Jay had apparently found another ride to soccer. I slammed around the kitchen, banging pots and pans in dinner preparation, then gave up, too drained to cook or think. Scotty had a late afternoon meeting anyway; we'd go out for pizza. *To celebrate,* I thought bitterly.

She found me on the small terrace behind our

house, thumbing through a dog-eared copy of *Writer's Market*, a thick reference sourcebook for ever-aspiring writers. Occasionally reading the entries beneath some obscure magazine seeking submissions, I turned the pages, studiously ignoring Ruth as she sat down wordlessly beside me on the rough brick steps.

"Pril," she finally said.

I kept my eyes on the fine print of the flimsy pages.

"What's your story about, Pril?"

I looked up, stared at the rubbed-raw patch of dirt beneath Sloan's swing. "Actually," I said, and spluttered a dull laugh, "it's about sex."

I sensed her faint smile. "Were you ruthless?" she asked.

My glance fell on the open page in my lap. "Here's a publication called *Nugget O'* that needs stories about 'B&D, TS, catfighting, spanking, fetishism, amputeeism, infantilism.' What do you suppose is 'TS'?"

"I don't know, Pril," she said. "I don't understand 'isms.' "

I closed the book. "Yes, you do. Feminism."

She put her hand on my knee. "Pril. I'm sorry, Pril. So sorry. For allowing the girls to see the breeding. It was wrong; you were right." She licked her lips, hesitating. "And I'm sorry for the low blow. You—"

"I deserved it. I overreacted, and I'm sorry. I behaved horribly. I was just so . . . so furious."

"I don't blame you," Ruth said. "It's all right. I understand. Particularly with what's being said about me." I looked at her questioningly, but she didn't notice, only took the volume from me and opened it. "Jesus." She laughed. "How appropriate. This magazine's called *On Our Backs: Entertainment for the Adventurous Lesbian.*"

"What are you talking about? What 'things' are being said?"

"You must not be spending enough time in carpool lines anymore."

"Don't joke, Ruth. What are you talking about?"

Ruth shook her head wearily, brushed hair from her eyes. "That I'm a lesbian. Or rather, that I've *become* a lesbian. Is that like a 'segue'?"

"A lesbian?" I demanded, stunned. The charge was patently ludicrous, but I couldn't laugh. "A lesbian," I repeated softly, wonderingly.

She sighed. "Maybe I am. Is there some lesbian litmus test, you think? I'm not repulsed by the thought of women together in bed. I don't feel like cutting my hair off, though wearing pants all the time has a definite appeal. Even my name is kind of butch, isn't it? *Ruth,*" she said. "Short and clipped."

"Shut up," I said. "That isn't funny, Ruth. Quit being flip."

"I know it's not funny. Reed doesn't find it very funny either. But what am I supposed to do? Denying the rumor would only give it credibility. It's not worth it. And who cares?" She shrugged. *"Pas moi."*

"Who would make up such a ridiculous—and vile—suggestion?" I offered, mentally casting about for a plausible perpetrator among our acquaintances. "Roslyn? Would Roslyn?"

Ruth traced her lips with her forefinger. "The entire concept is probably alien to Roslyn. She's too knee-deep in testosterone." Ruth shook her head. "Poor Roslyn. No, not her. I told you long ago she's harmless. It's Posey Caldwell and that tennis bunch. They see me at the stables when they bring their daughters for riding lessons on Thursdays."

"I know that crowd. They're . . . I don't know, downright dangerous."

Ruth smiled. "I'd rather be controversial than dangerous."

We were quiet a moment. I remembered the whispered assurances years ago at camp, how Ruth Sloan was at Kiahwassee for both sessions because her parents wanted to get rid of her, didn't love her. "I had a roommate in college who's become a militant lesbian. She listened to Tammy Wynette and had her face peeled one vacation. She used to pay me to pick up her clothes from the floor."

"Listen to that perfect memory for detail," Ruth said admiringly.

"I get Christmas cards from her asking me when I'm going to 'acknowledge' her. I haven't figured out what she means."

"A speaker came to our group the other night," Ruth said, "a counselor for women who discover they're lesbians after they marry and have children."

She handed me my wrinkled letter of acceptance. "But I missed the session."

A slowly dawning truth opened before me—the countless hours and days and years Ruth and I spent in one another's company, in one another's confidence. "So I guess the rumors include me too," I said, amused. "Your *partner* in sexual scandal. I'm the last to hear about myself." I tapped her shoulder, adding lightly. "Don't worry. We'll ride them out."

It was Ruth's turn to be surprised. "Oh no, Pril," she said. "You're not the one they've paired me with. Not you." She stretched her legs. "It's Naomi."

Somewhere in the park a child's voice, high and hopeful and plaintive, called out. "Aussie!" it sounded like, falling off a note at the second syllable. A male voice followed—"Aussie!"—the father.

"Lost dog," Ruth commented. I said nothing, stilled, quiet, and for the second time that day, speechless. Mute not with disgust or chagrin or surprise at the unfair accusation directed at my friend, but with recognition of a distinct disappointment; a pointed personal wounding that it was Naomi Ruth was linked to. Naomi, instead of me.

Chapter 7

D id Mr. Campbell mistreat Mrs. Campbell in any way, Mrs. Henderson."

"Of course not."

With my answer Reed smiled broadly, as though I had unwittingly given him an extravagant compliment.

"Define 'mistreatment,'" I could have said; but it wasn't the issue here. Ruth and I both had already been witnesses to mistreatment.

The year Bethie turned eleven, Jay turned fourteen, and I turned thirty-nine, Berk left Roslyn. For years every morning Berk had driven away, leaving Roslyn praying it wouldn't be the day God sent a fateful wreck the way of his commute. Who can judge which tragedy would have been preferable?

I watched him leave; watched him hoist a duffle

into the car trunk for another weekend hunting trip, I assumed, another "opening day" somewhere, and registered no small envy for Roslyn's solitude. It was an afternoon in early fall, the park trees still full but tiredly green, the broad leaves of the Lawrences' magnolia lusterless with September dust. I stood in the doorway admiring a certain beauty in the gentle curves of our deliberately brittled, blighted lawn. On an earlier weekend we had all sprayed our yards with a lethal chemical in preparation for reseeding. "The Big Kill," Reed joked about the process as he and Scotty strapped surgical masks over their mouths and noses. "Greenus envy," Ruth had declared. By the time Berk left, infant threads of green had begun to sprout, poking bravely through the flattened mat of dead grass.

It was the next week before she told us; before, perhaps, the shock allowed her to admit it even to herself. Shooing the curious children from Ruth's kitchen, we poured coffee and listened to her stilted, stammered story. Beneath her eyes lay shadows of fatigue and crying.

Ruth advocated instant action. "Roslyn, you've got to get a lawyer, pronto."

"A lawyer?" Roslyn shook her head. "Berk just wants a little time, some temporary 'space.'"

"Where did he go?" I asked. "Where's he going to live?"

"I don't know," she confessed. "An apartment." She stripped a hardened cuticle from an otherwise perfectly manicured fingernail. "It's not so different, is it? He was never here before, was he?"

"Roslyn," Ruth said, "listen to me. You put a private investigator on Berk's butt and slap him with an abandonment and adultery suit for every penny he's worth."

Roslyn was visibly aghast. "Ruth. This is only a little midlife crisis. He's just temporarily restless. The children are gone, at college, working, Berk's had the same job since he was twenty-four—"

"Why, has he quit his job?" I interrupted.

"No, actually, he just got a big promotion—but you know what a workaholic he is. He just needs some time to reassess. I can understand that, can't you?" She waited for our agreement. I swallowed. Ruth drummed her fingers on the table.

"I should've gotten a job," Roslyn said. "Berk's been after me for months to do something that brings home a paycheck."

A knowing look crossed Ruth's face. "Don't do it, Roslyn."

"Well, he's right. I'm perfectly capable."

"And that's precisely what he's trying to prove, and will, in court. That you're capable of earning your own living so he won't have to support you."

But Roslyn wasn't listening. "Berk didn't say he wasn't coming back. He didn't say he didn't . . ."— she hesitated—"love me." A small whimper escaped her throat. "I don't want to do anything drastic. Anything that would make him mad. If I'm nice, maybe he'll come home." Her voice was pained with tragic confusion and wondering naïveté. "I thought it was supposed to be smooth sailing, now that we've finished all the difficult parts."

"Son of a bitch," Ruth said, unmoved and undeterred. "That son of a bitch."

"What can we do?" I asked helplessly. "What do you need?"

Roslyn smiled faintly. "Nothing. This too will pass. I'm like Anne Frank. I still believe that people are really good at heart."

"Quit quoting those platitudes!" Ruth thundered.

Roslyn ignored her. "When Berk gets home I'll have everything waiting for him," she said. "Perfect and organized."

Ruth took Roslyn's hand in her own and stroked it. "Roslyn," she said simply, "when have you not been perfect and organized?"

For a week Roslyn's cheerfulness was unbounded, her faith in Berk's return undaunted. Her days seemed to be filled with frenzied bursts of determined busyness, and she waved gaily from the porch as she washed windows, from the car as she passed to and from domestic errands. At night every window of the house blazed with hospitable, welcoming warmth. Heartened, Ruth and I crossed the park to share our Friday afternoon glass of wine with Roslyn. We found her, slump-shouldered and slovenly, near the garage. At our approach she looked up, a terrible, defeated despair etched on her face.

"What is it?" I asked, alarmed. "Have you heard from Berk?"

"No," she said quietly, then "yes." She held out a catalog, furled tightly as a newspaper where she had continually kneaded it. "I found this in a stack of his hunting supply magazines." I unrolled it, a Victoria's Secret catalog featuring page after page of long-haired, long-legged lingerie models. "At the top," Roslyn whispered, "in the corner."

A pouting bikini-clad brunette lounging on pink satin sheets gazed provocatively from the page. Her breasts bulged like fleshy melons from a tiny black lace bra, no differently than dozens of other seductive poses. But beneath the photograph, in bold black damning strokes, was scribbled, *"Trina. Order this."*

"Trina," Roslyn repeated dully. " 'Trina, order this.' Do you know who Trina is? Short for Katrina. Berk's pet name for our yard woman! Isn't that rich?" Her voice rose to a screech. "My husband is having an affair with the blond braid who cuts our grass! I was the one who hired her all those years ago, when she was eighteen, out of college, broke! And now . . ." The shriek broke into sobbing. "I believed him!" she cried. "All those nights he said he was working, all those afternoons and weekends he said he was hunting, I believed him." She collapsed to her knees, covering her face with her hands. "He never had a nickname for me!" she cried piteously. "All these years I have tried to do everything right, to be a good wife. A good mother. I tried so hard," she moaned softly. "So so hard. What didn't I do right?"

Ruth knelt swiftly beside her and pulled her hands away. "Roslyn," she said. "You *are* a good mother. You're a wonderful wife. It's nothing *you* did, Roslyn. It's what Berk did, Berk! This is not your fault."

Roslyn seemed not to hear. She reached out and stroked the fine threads of new grass, wispy strands of tender green. "Look," she said, touching a swerved hardened rut beside the driveway. "I'm always careful when I reverse. So careful." Her voice cracked again. "He ran over the baby grass. He killed it." But when she spoke again, her voice was gritty and tough. "The shithead," she said, Roslyn, whom I'd never heard utter a profanity. "No wonder we were paying that bitch so goddamn much. Somebody had to support their fuckfests."

The abrupt, unnerving change of attitude was a prelude; a prelude to the coming weeks in which, like the season and the leaves, Roslyn disintegrated and withered by degrees. She had always been beyond us, separate, apart, finished with the needs and rituals of children, but in those distraught, distressing weeks that followed, Ruth and I found ourselves thrust into Roslyn's life. Out of sympathy, out of proximity, out of necessity. And because we were women.

We invited and included her in family functions and excursions, the school's fall bazaar, movies and meals out, soccer games. Nearly always she declined.

The few occasions she agreed to accompany us, we tried to ignore the shock on our children's faces at how pert, pressed, sunny-demeanored Roslyn had become straggle-haired and morose. There was no elaborately carved Halloween pumpkin on the Lawrence steps that October; no piles of leaves she raked especially for the children to jump in. The leaves lay where they fell, blotting the thickening grass, strewn like paper scraps on the wide porch.

"The Rogaine," Roslyn announced to no one during Jay's soccer game we'd persuaded her to attend with us.

I turned to her on the bleacher. "What?"

Roslyn nodded sagely, plucking her sleeve. "I should've guessed. The Rogaine prescription to grow his hair. He's been trying to grow hair for six months, right here." She touched the crown of her head. "It's very expensive medicine."

Scotty and I exchanged nervous glances. "Anybody want a Coke?" he queried. "I'm going to the concession stand." Roslyn only stared at the field, unresponsive.

I confronted Scotty afterward. "Did you know?" I accused, never dreaming the question would soon be asked of me. "*Did you know?* Did you know Berk was going to leave?"

"Of course not, Pril. I'm as stunned as you."

"Would you have told me if you did?"

He looked at me. "What's the issue here? Are you thinking of Roslyn or yourself? Ruth, or someone, has given you an exaggerated idea of how much men talk. Give Roslyn some time. It's like a death. She has to go through the stages of grief before she can accept it."

I was irked by his penny psychology. "It's worse than death. It's rejection."

"Would you rather Berk be dead, then?" he shot back, and I could only clamp my jaw shut, strangled with the injustice.

But there was no progressive pattern to Roslyn's behavior, no healing stages of shock, denial, grief, anger. By erratic turns she was disturbingly docile, then frighteningly hostile. During pitiful confessional interludes of self-loathing and self-recrimination, she would suddenly revert to vicious, biting irrationality. She vacillated between limitless childlike faith in Berk's eventual return and caustic stinging cynicism. But after each rash outburst or tearful entreaty she returned to the same unanswerable question: *Why?*

Some weekends, thankfully, her sons came, William and Trey and David, the trio of boys, now men in their twenties, I scarcely knew. They had matured, grown into lanky, shuffling versions of their father, but still helpless in the face of their shattered family: one parent altered, the other absent.

"How are the boys doing?" I asked after one visit.

Roslyn stared vacantly over her backyard, the carefully tended perennial border felled by frost and left to decay. "For the first time in my life, I'm glad they're grown up. They've all just had birthdays," she said. "I sent belts. Berk sent money. With which David bought himself a fire-breathing dragon down his forearm to celebrate turning twenty-one." She passed her palm absently over her lips.

Ruth's eyes widened. "A tattoo?" I asked.

She looked up at me indignantly. "Well, didn't I say that?" Her voice sank to a lackadaisical murmur. "Of course, I was the one who always handled the birthdays." She giggled, and a maniacal hilarity fringed her laughter. "I delivered three babies during the World Series. A television squawked in every room of the hospital, including mine." She stroked her cheek, grew serious. "But that isn't nearly so remarkable as the fact that I was screwing so seriously, so goddamn *intently* in January. When I was trying to get pregnant, Berk would go in the bathroom and clean himself up," she said with thick tonelessness, "and I would lie in bed with my legs up in the air so his sperm wouldn't drain out of me."

I turned away, shutting my eyes to the vision she conjured. *Don't tell me!* I thought desperately; *Don't!*

Berk's severance was shamelessly final. Except for impersonal legal missives, he never contacted Roslyn. But in a fugue of despondency, she stooped to phoning Trina. A young girl answered, innocently saying, as she had no doubt been instructed to when a parent wasn't home, "She's in the shower."

Roslyn scowled in disbelief at the receiver. "Then let me speak to your father," she demanded poisonously. "He's in the shower, too," the child duly responded. "You have another think if you think my husband's going to support someone else's brat!" Roslyn yelled into the phone.

Had it been any other circumstance, we might have laughed. "Calm down, Roslyn!" Ruth said. "It's a child, for God's sake."

She turned on us both with steely menace. "Child! *Her* child! Who I didn't know existed! Now you shut up quoting platitudes to *me*. It's not Reed's dick poking someone else. When you have notes to compare, we'll talk." Yet within minutes, the unhinged wrath ricocheted to embarrassing sentimentality.

"Why did I say that? She'll tell Berk. I want to be good. I want him to come back."

"*Why?*" Ruth exclaimed, suppressing an astonished shriek. "He's treated you terribly."

"Because I still love him," Roslyn answered with tragically naked honesty. "What will I do? What will I be?"

Ruth and I waited and watched and worried. As the machinery of legal separation ground inexorably forward, papers arrived for Roslyn's signature. The terms were blatantly unfair, stinking of premeditated deceit. Berk's proposed "support" was paltry, based on his salary before the six-figure promotion at work. Neither Trey's law school expenses nor David's remaining year at college were included. Charge card balances, car payments, doctor and dentist and insurance payments were all left to Roslyn. And yet it was with confusion and incomprehension, not anger, that

Roslyn questioned the documents. "Can they do this? Do I have to sign? Can they make me? How can we have an 'agreement' when I don't agree?" Her innocence was staggering.

Reed finally convinced Roslyn to hire an attorney, but it took three weeks to find someone to represent her. The only lawyers whose names she vaguely knew refused, even Reed and Scotty's recommendations, on the grounds of knowing Berk personally or professionally. "Brick walls!" Roslyn fumed after another negative answer. "Of course the idiots 'know' us! How else would I know *them*? Ruth is right. It's all shit for women. Shit!" And swiftly as the tantrum had come over her, it subsided to a plaintive bewildered bleating, an endless search for reasons and justification. "I never ran the washing machine when he took a shower, so he would have enough hot water. I always had meals ready. He never ran out of clean socks. I changed the batteries in the smoke detector. I tried not to wear the same clothes twice in one week."

"This is what happens when a woman has no definition of herself, when her sole security stems from her husband and her children and her home," Ruth said. "She's totally vulnerable. Roslyn has nothing to lean on but herself, and 'herself' is Berk's wife. She can't fathom a future without him."

"Oh, Ruth," I said, "can't you step down from the feminist soapbox for a minute?"

But it was Ruth who found Frances Shelley, an attorney suggested by a member of her women's group. "But how will I pay?" Roslyn asked.

"Berk will pay," Ruth assured her.

One cold afternoon I found Roslyn on my front steps clutching a tattered wicker box of old photographs.

"Why are you out here without a coat?" I asked. "The house is unlocked; come on in."

She only tightened her grasp on the box. "Do you have any pictures of Scotty touching you?" she asked. "Of him holding you, like this?" She stood and placed her icy palms on my cheeks, cupping my face in her hands.

"I don't think so," I said, taking her hands in mine. "Please, Roslyn. Come inside where it's warm and have some coffee."

Tears welled in her eyes. "Neither do I," she said. "You should take some pictures like that," she said simply, turning to leave. "Someday you might want them."

The unpredictable swings of temperament, of self-delusion alternating with despair, were terrifying, and Ruth and I worried privately about Roslyn's mental stability. "She's struggling for her sanity," Ruth said. "I'm afraid she's having a nervous breakdown."

"Is it depression?" I wondered, with my scant knowledge of the condition. "But half the time she's too energized by fury to be clinically depressed."

"We've got to get her to a psychiatrist."

"But how? We can't just commit her, drag her off in a straightjacket."

"We can't look to her parents for help, either," Ruth agreed. "Her mother's dead, and her father's in a nursing home in Michigan." We suggested a counselor to the boys, and solicited the help of our husbands, who went to talk with Roslyn individually too. But none of them saw any of the rash erratic behavior Ruth and I had personally witnessed. "I think when Roslyn's with a man, any man," Ruth surmised, "she unconsciously puts on an act, reverts to an ultrafeminine helpmeet, maternal persona. It's always worked for her. This thing is pushing her over the edge."

"You need to talk to someone, Roslyn." Ruth finally confronted her.

"I'm talking to you," she answered dully.

"Not me and Pril. A professional. A counselor who can help you get through this. You can't do it by yourself." A thought crossed Ruth's mind. "Have you been keeping your appointments with Frances? What does she say?"

But Roslyn had already ceased to listen. "I think I could stand it," she said. "I think I could bear it if he would just leave." She looked at us to make sure we understood. "Not leave me. He's already done that, right?" She laughed dispiritedly. "I mean leave Greensboro. If he would just go away and live somewhere else."

But Roslyn's deepest degradation was yet to come,

at Thanksgiving. She called me the Wednesday morning before. "My boys are coming tomorrow."

"Wonderful!" I said, standing in the kitchen amid the mess of my own holiday preparations. "Are you cooking or going out?"

"Pril, I . . ." At the other end of the line her voice faltered and cracked. "I don't have any money for groceries. I need to borrow a hundred dollars." I tried to muffle my gasp of shock. "He's not going to come back to me, is he?" she said with pathetic clarity. "Does this qualify as rock bottom?"

Finally Roslyn signed the separation agreement, convinced by Frances Shelley that it was neither conclusive nor binding, and that acquiescence was her only immediate recourse for funds. And then, two weeks before Christmas, Roslyn seemed to partially recover. She went to see her church rector, who offered her a part-time job at the church's library. Pleasure suffused her face when Roslyn presented her first paycheck to us.

"Nine dollars an hour!" She beamed. "Know what I typed on my résumé under 'work history'? I put 'meaningful experience.' " She looked away, suddenly unreachable again. "It's nice in the library. Quiet. No one ever comes. There are lots of books for, for . . . people like me."

As the holiday season shifted into high gear, something of Roslyn's old spark returned, and Ruth and I were encouraged by the apparent rebound. "This Christmas," Roslyn announced, "I'm getting a Fraser fir. For twenty-three years Berk insisted on cedars, those old branches that can't hold a decent ornament. Flimsy as feathers. Flimsy as my marriage! And I'll have little white lights too, not those big globby blue and orange ones Berk always wanted. What was I thinking all those years, decorating for Berk?"

"Sure," Ruth enthusiastically agreed. "Look at it this way. You're finally free."

Roslyn looked up at her. "But that's just it," she corrected. "I never wanted to be free."

"Look," I said too quickly, too brightly. "Ruth and I always make our wreaths together. You come too, keep a lookout while we steal boxwood and nandina from the park."

And so she did, watching lethargically as we assembled our wreaths. She flipped through my Christmas cards, collected in a basket whose stitched "Merry Christmas" panel she'd needlepointed herself as a gift to us an earlier year. "Seems ex-wives are pariahs for parties," she noted, studying party invitations I'd thoughtlessly tossed in with the happy family greeting cards.

I changed the subject. "Ruth and I always have a tackiest card contest. Here's my choice." I held up a felt-flocked horror from a business associate of Scotty's, which pictured a fat red candle glowing ethereally on a bed of fake holly, complete with open Bible and satin bookmark.

"No way," Ruth countered. "This one." She selected a mimeographed letter, long typewritten paragraphs describing a year's worth of family trips and events, children's scholastic and sports achievements. "What an insulting bore."

"I couldn't bring myself to do a card this year," Roslyn said. "What would I write? 'This year my husband left me for a woman who drives a tractor mower. I have a thrilling new job as a librarian, no, as a "media specialist" in a one-room church library. My middle son has a fire-breathing dragon tattoo on his forearm. And oh, yes, the flames are infected.' "

Ruth laughed feebly. "Don't, Roslyn."

"Don't what?" she returned with forced cheerfulness. "Don't tell the truth or don't tell you?"

She asked Bethie and Sloan to bake cookies and make ornaments. "You're so lucky to have girls," she said to Ruth and me. "I wanted one." She looked up quickly, swift to deny any implied suggestion that she didn't love her boys. "Naturally I didn't have a third baby because I expected a girl. But I hoped with three boys that *someone* would come and visit me in my old age." When she subsequently invited the girls to make candles of spray-painted paper towel tubes and dried magnolia pods, they complained that they were too old for such kindergarten crafts, but Ruth and I insisted they go.

Christmas Day dawned disappointingly sunny and mild. Scotty and I left with the children that afternoon for four intensive days of family rounds, the interval between Christmas and New Year's when someone else's sorrow takes second stage. Ruth and Reed left town as well, staying through the New Year's weekend in Reed's hometown for a black-tie party. On New Year's Eve a cold pelting rain set in; Scotty and I were content to celebrate with a rented video. We went to bed long before midnight, leaving the children to televised Times Square and sparkling grape juice.

At a gloomy twilight a day later, I was searching halfheartedly through the stuffed trash bin at the curb for instructions inadvertently thrown away, when Ruth appeared, dragging her denuded Christmas tree. Waiting for the city trash rounds, discarded Christmas trees dotted the neighborhood streets. Like prostrate pantalooned Southern belles, the trees lay with their framework of branches exposed. Bereft of their finery, the pretty evergreens that had so recently been carefully selected and decorated, given exalted living room status, were now no better than curbside detritus, bread wrappers.

"Sad sight, isn't it?" Ruth observed by way of greeting. "Bet the Neatniks have had their tree out since the day after Christmas."

"How was the soiree?" I asked.

She plucked a silvery icicle from the tree's branches and wrapped it tightly around her thumb. "Remember being thrilled to see your name penned in beautiful calligraphy script on a place card at a fancy party? Remember? There was a time when I would have taken that little card, that epitome of elegance and glamour, home in my pocketbook to save and take out and look at. A little souvenir of sophistication." She pulled her coat tightly to her body, turning up the felt collar. "Did you make any resolutions?"

"Are you going soft on me, Ruth?" We'd always agreed that resolutions were catalysts for failure. When she didn't respond, I said, "Scotty made one for me."

That got her attention. "Scotty? Since when do you allow him to make your resolutions?"

I shrugged. "Actually, it was kind of sweet. He wants me to stop and smell the flowers this year, to not be so anxious for the next thing to happen. The next day, the next letter, the next story."

Ruth nodded. A ghostly creeping mist hovered below us in the valley, where recent rains had resurrected the trickle of creek. Across the park the imposing edifice of the Lawrence house stood squarely, now no more than a grand vacant facade. "It's funny," Roslyn had recently said with no trace of humor, "in those early years, when you're trapped in your house with babies, all you want is to have it tidy and decorated. But when they're gone, and you finally have the time and energy to get it right, why then you don't care any longer. It's funny."

As Ruth and I silently watched the house, the overhead porch light suddenly flicked on, casting its puny glow over Roslyn's purchased wreath, now a crisp circular carcass.

"The cards are stacked for Roslyn," Ruth said. "He gets the girl, and he gets the money, and he gets the new life. They always have been. They're stacked for you and me too."

"It's a new year," I countered. "Roslyn's doing so much better. She'll be okay. What's that line from Shakespeare? 'People have died from time to time, and worms have eaten them, but not for love.'"

"It's 'men,'" Ruth said. "'*Men* have died from time to time, but not for love.'"

"Roslyn will survive," I stubbornly asserted.

"I don't know," Ruth said slowly. "I'm not sure."

I blew on my hands to warm them. "Why did you ask about my resolution? Did you and Reed make any?"

"I did."

"And?"

Ruth paused, exhaled a long sigh. "I resolved never to wake up again relying on someone else for my happiness. I am never going to be blindsided by love for someone, or lack of it. Never never will I be that vulnerable."

I watched her, the specter of the taunt I'd flung years earlier at the stables rising between us, suspended and wraithlike. "But Ruth, marriage—any relationship—is about linking your happiness and well-being to someone else. About caring for someone else as much as you care for yourself. You yield some measure of independence because you want to. How do you separate someone else's happiness from your own? How do you extract it without hurting someone?"

"Oh, Pril!" Ruth said. Puffs of white steam punctuated her words. "You expect happy endings. How can you be a writer and go on believing in happy endings?"

I looked down and shivered, toeing the fragile fallen pine needles littering the asphalt. With runny noses and hands shoved in our pockets, we stood there together as darkness descended, a damp chill seeping through our coats. The long months of winter, bleak and bare, heartless and housebound, lay before us like a sentence. "You didn't answer my question," I said finally, stubbornly. "If you love someone, can your happiness exist apart from theirs?"

"I don't know, Pril," Ruth said again, her answer surely an unintentional repetition of her earlier response. "I'm not sure."

Chapter 8

Ruth telephoned one morning in late January. "Locate your calendar," she said. "Let's get out of Dodge."

"Great," I said, delighted. "We're due." We'd taken three- or four-day getaways together through the years, just the two of us; for deserted beaches in off-season Marches, for mountain hikes during leaf season, for days of museum wanderings and evenings of theater in Washington. But neither destination nor weather nor entertainment were the reasons behind the trips. We went to purely relax, to flee the requirements and responsibilities and schedules of motherhood, wifedom, and household. They were treasured times: unaccountable, unorganized, unorchestrated liberty. We giggled and lounged like lazy adolescents, gossiped like crones, waged debates and discussions, or simply reveled in an utter quiet no child could disturb. Or spouse, for that matter. "Complete pelvic rest," Ruth once wryly described our trips. Laden with books and magazines, liquor and music, even movies if a VCR was available, we simply drove away, leaving behind lengthy memos with Reed and Scotty about children's activities and substitute carpools, emergency numbers and precooked meals. "When and where?" I asked.

Ruth hesitated. "How about this week?" When I paused she continued in a rush of resolve. "This is seriously spur-of-the-minute, but I read about a little bed-and-breakfast outside Asheville, and they have vacancies. I made a reservation for Tuesday and Wednesday nights. Would that be okay?"

"Sure." I agreed, surprised. Usually we decided jointly when and where to go, allowing plenty of time for anticipation as part of the enjoyment. "Let me check with Scotty. I don't think any catastrophes are slated for this week."

Ruth drove. We talked little, relishing the prospect of hours and hours without obligation. With the car heater's breathy warmth on my toes, I was content with watching the winter-shorn landscape segue into fir-covered foothills. After three hours the sharper, harsher vistas of rocky peaks dominated the horizon, and the benign gray ribbon of interstate spiraled, requiring low gear. Lacy remnants of earlier snows clung to curbs and hid in the shadows of roadside boulders. Mere feet beyond my window, perpendicular rock walls were glazed blue-gray with diminutive waterfalls frozen in their trickled tracks.

The slender brochure for Mallow Ridge Lodge had promised a charming, cozy retreat. Even from the outside we weren't disappointed, despite the up-ended wooden rockers on the wraparound porch, the chains dangling forlornly from the overhang, bereft of their hanging flower baskets. A converted summer home, the Lodge was perched on a broad outcropping of rock overlooking a precipitous drop into a steep wooded gorge.

"Don't get too many visitors this time of year," Mr. Hodgin, the owner, mused as he showed us to our room and busied himself with lighting a fire in the small stone fireplace. He stood and brushed his hands against his pants. "You gals running away?" He chuckled. "That's what I did. Ran away from a chain of New Jersey hardware stores three years ago and never looked back. No regrets, no ma'am. You ever want to open an inn, I'm the one to talk to." Ruth and I smiled, indulging his garrulous kindness, the Yankee twang. "Well," he said, "I'll just leave you this list of restaurants in the area, got a local diner that cooks up the best waffles in the state." I nodded politely. Fast food, four-star, or dingy diner, it didn't matter. What mattered was not cooking ourselves. "You sure you don't want two rooms?" he asked. "Give you some room to spread out. Got one just as nice across the hall."

"Oh, no," I assured him. "We always share a

room." He looked doubtfully at us and backed out the door. I giggled at whatever conclusions he was drawing, then flung back the heavy coverlet of the bed and threw myself across its sheeted expanse. "First things first," I said, stretching luxuriously. "*Now* it feels like vacation. Nothing like a deliberately unmade bed in the middle of the day for living dangerously and decadently."

"Actually, I almost got us separate rooms," Ruth said.

"What?" I demanded with mock indignation. We'd always ridiculed our husbands' adamant refusal to share beds with other men. "Why? It's amazing how in college men have no qualms about goosing each other and getting drunk and tearing each other's clothes off, but with graduation some homophobic terror hormone kicks in. Promise me we'll never do that, Ruth, never get too adult or too modest or too whatever to share rooms."

Ruth smiled at me and picked up a piece of china bric-a-brac lining the planked mantel. Besides the beds, the room held a rocking chair and stubby oak bureau with a fringed dresser scarf. I walked to the window flanking the fireplace and pulled back the curtain panel of sheer scalloped lace. With precisely pointed tips like sharpened pencils, tall spindly pines were eye-level from our window. The winter day was achingly clear and still. No birds, no falling leaves, not even clouds marred the vast visual peace. With their dense blanket of evergreens, minor mountain ranges nearby looked like a carelessly gathered quilt of chenille. The horizon was a velvet swath, where the ancient, majestic Blue Ridge accumulated ridge after ridge in great, gentle multiplying folds and shades of gray-blue.

"There's something nearly erotic about that view, the way one range humps to the next," I said. The fire crackled behind me, the lit room already comfortably cluttered with our belongings. "Should we call home and let them know we made it?"

Ruth pulled a worn flannel nightgown from her bag. "Let's make a pact not to call home."

"Deal," I agreed in delicious lawless collusion. "Even though I know I'm indispensable."

"Do you really think that?" Ruth asked. I glanced at her. She'd been strangely subdued thus far, for Ruth, distant and nearly guarded. I'd dismissed it as driving concentration, but some unnatural reserve still clung to her.

"What'll we do first?" I asked, ignoring her rhetorical question. "There's a used-book store called Pages in Asheville I've always wanted to see. I've still got some Christmas cash to spend. Would you mind going?"

We wound outside the small hamlet that constituted the Mallow Ridge community, undiscovered by commerce but for two or three stores offering a queer combination of common necessities and useless luxuries: imported soaps, acrylic ice buckets, Italian china. "For the upscale summer trade," Ruth speculated as we passed cottages shuttered to the winter season. But occasionally, tucked behind leafy privacy hedges of rhododendron and mountain laurel we glimpsed thin snaking trails of smoke from the fire of a permanent resident.

"Wouldn't it be lovely to live here year-round? Away from civilization," I murmured. "A writer's dream, all this solitude." I tapped Ruth on the shoulder. "Wouldn't I make a great recluse?"

Ruth only smiled without taking her eyes from the road. "You could never do that, Pril."

I was annoyed by her contradiction, however well-intentioned, however correct. "Why not?"

"Because," she said. "You need people too much. Don't you recognize that by now?" As I gnawed a cold finger, debating her assessment, she gentled her rebuke. "You need people to watch. Who would you watch?"

Before us, dozens of perfectly aligned, perfectly conical young fir trees marched in rows up the steep mountainside like attentive soldiers. I thought of Roslyn and her Christmas Fraser fir. Some semblance of routine and normalcy had settled over our neighbor's life since the low point of Thanksgiving. She was seeing an analyst regularly, if not altogether enthusiastically, and had joined a support group who called themselves EGBAR, an acronym for "Everything's Gonna Be All Right." "Should we have invited Roslyn, you think?" I asked idly.

"Her boys are coming this weekend," Ruth said.

"She has something to look forward to. Here it is— Pages."

We entered the etched glass doors of the used-book store, and I breathed deeply of the intoxicating scents of old paper and ink. A bar in another era, the building was narrow with high ceilings and slatted wood floors that had never known wax, only brooms. An age-mottled mirror behind the bar was pasted with enlarged and laminated book jacket re-productions, with the muted colors and dated script of the twenties and thirties. Easels, tables, and narrow drawers held fragile documents: antique maps, parchment deeds, and bills of sale for land and slaves and dry goods, banded Confederate currency useful to no one but collectors.

And the books . . . Shelf upon shelf of volumes, the very rows eliciting a familiar literary dread and yearning within me. I ran my fingers over the spines, the titles both familiar and obscure, drawing no distinction in value between the stiff or supple leather bindings, the clear Mylar casings that preserved irre-placeable original jackets, and the plain, humble hardbacks. I had no mantra of must-haves or interest in collecting for investment, aspired to possess no uniquely valuable autographed first edition. It was enough to browse and touch and savor, to locate titles of books once or still significant to me. Now and then I pulled an anthology from the shelf, automati-cally checking the acknowledgment pages to see where the stories had first been published, in periodicals both famed and defunct.

Toward the end of the alphabetical listing, I paused at a particular book and held it, clearly recalling the anguish with which I had finished its last powerful pages.

"What's that?" Ruth asked over my shoulder. I held the book up. "*All the Little Live Things,*" she read. "Wallace Stegner. Have you read it?"

I nodded. "It's about a couple who believe they're happily married, content, and serene and secure, and this outsider, this third party arrives, and violates . . ." I trailed off, remembering the brutal concluding scene. "It's a first edition, with the original jacket, and the author is deceased." I flipped to the front and checked the faintly penciled price. "One hundred and twenty-five dollars."

Ruth whistled. "Go ahead and get it." I shook my head. "Why not?"

"I can't rationalize buying it."

Ruth gave me an appraising look, and sighed impatiently. "So what? Do you always need a reason, Pril?" I flattened my palm against the smooth coolness of the cover, dimly reflecting our expressions, mine tentative, Ruth's definite. "I suppose I do," I said, and replaced the book in its slot.

We followed Mr. Hodgin's suggestion for dinner at The Highland House, a predictably Scottish-themed restaurant decorated with carved crests and heraldic coats of arms, tartan linens and plaid rugs. The waiter took our order for broiled mountain trout, and with glasses of wine and the bottle iced beside us, I sat back and gazed around the room, surprisingly full for a midwinter weeknight. Sheer habit compelled me to assign names, personalities, and histories to strangers I would never see again.

"What'll we do tomorrow?" I asked, not really expecting an answer. The joy of our journeys lay in the absence of plans. "The Craft Guild? But how many crockery pitchers can you own? What about the Biltmore Mansion?" I proposed, quashing a twinge of guilt for not bringing the children to tour the famous castle.

"I've made plans for tomorrow," Ruth said quietly. "An appointment."

"What?" I asked, still absorbed in other patrons' probable lives. "You know, I can attach a history to every person in this room. That's the simple part, narrative. Fabricating what happens is easy. It's the motivations that are difficult."

Ruth gazed serenely at me. "There you are again, with your reasons."

"Look at that pregnant woman. She must be eight months plus. Remember that?" I went glibly on. "Remember feeling bulky and bloated and oafish, like a cow dressed in a denim jumper? You're right, Ruth. Some male made up that fairy tale about pregnant women 'glowing.' There's nothing like some man saying 'How you feel, honey?' to incite you to blows." I laughed. "Remember?" I raised my glass.

"A toast to our dual tubals." In the face of our husbands' staunch refusals, four years earlier we'd both undergone laparoscopic surgeries to tie our tubes, and nursed each other through a weekend of distended abdomens and tender navels. Since then we'd joked that if we had another baby, we'd also have a lawsuit.

"I remember, Pril." The studied quietness of Ruth's tone pulled me back to her. "I remember because I am."

Fork halted midway to my mouth, I dropped my eyes to the table's edge, her belly. "Am what?"

She nodded, her eyes fixed on mine. "At the moment."

I barely heard her. "But that's impossible."

"I'm also a statistic. About one in five hundred."

I put down the fork. "Well. Reed must certainly be strutting. Mr. Super Sperm."

"Reed doesn't know," Ruth said. I glanced up swiftly, my surprise renewed. "Do you think I'd have come all the way up here if he knew?" she said. "If I thought he would agree?" She gripped the edge of the table with both hands. "Do you understand me, Pril? I have an appointment tomorrow at nine thirty. For an abortion."

"Why?"

"*Why?*" Ruth repeated. "I'm pregnant," she repeated with measured severity. "Which reason would you like to begin with? Though I'll warn you, I've already been through the required hour of counseling." She traced the rim of her wine goblet with her finger.

There was no sarcasm, no defensiveness, no tremor to her voice or crack in the armor of her decision. I stared at her, stunned by her air of calm indifference. I thought of Reed, who in years past had talked of having another child; of Roslyn, who in happier days had extolled with near braggadocio the pleasures and advantages of three children. And I thought of Scotty, who was so strongly opposed to abortion on moral grounds that we never broached the topic outside of campaign years and candidates' promises. Never discussed it because I believed so strongly that a woman had the right to do with her body as she pleased, and suffer the consequences— moral or physical. But this was different. This was personal. This was Ruth, and I felt my convictions tumbling. "Ruth, I . . . Don't you want to wait and see? Have you had an amnio?"

"Wait and see what? I'm not quite nine weeks along." Beneath the table I twisted the napkin around my knuckles. "I'm forty-four, Pril."

"People have babies at forty-four," I said. "And Sloan, think of it, you'd have a built-in sitter. Wouldn't she be thrilled?" Words bubbled from my lips. "And Reed, he—"

Ruth shook her head, forestalling my protests. "No, Pril." She reached across the table, then stopped. "This isn't about morality."

"I know that!" I insisted vehemently. "Have I

mentioned that? I haven't!" Other diners looked our way, and I lowered my voice. "Think of it. You could start over. And Roslyn has always implied that we've missed something, or were inferior in some way, the both of us, having only two children."

"Roslyn," Ruth said, shaking her head. "Has it ever occurred to her we were just smart enough to *stop*? I was not the third-child princess. I was the third-child mistake."

I bit my lip. "But Ruth, the odds were so high against your getting pregnant. . . . Your tubes are tied. Have you considered that this pregnancy, this child, is just . . . meant to be? Fated to be born?" I reached for her hand, but it lay motionless on the tablecloth. "I'm just trying to be fair."

Ruth gazed at me over her wine for a long un-comfortable moment. "This is not about fairness. It is not about starting over. It is not about what is best for Reed or the children, or the . . . or the fetus." The clinical term was shockingly sterile. When she spoke again, her voice was strong with emphasis. "It's about what's best for me. For me, Pril. It's my choice."

I looked down at my plate, the food grown chilled and congealed. "Pril, look at me," Ruth said. Her eyes were pleading. "I cannot be burdened with an-other . . . person. Answer me, Pril. Would you start over? Could you?"

I knew what she was asking me. She was asking me about twenty years of commitment and responsibility. The issue of giving oneself to another in every positive and negative aspect lay plainly between us, an enormously selfish issue. More enormous, more significant than the possibility of producing an individual who might contribute to humankind in a thousand unknown ways. More enormous than the issue of safety or choice or consequences. But more significant than the opportunity to love? The ability to create? There it lay, naked as a newborn, naked as the truth. "No," I whispered, shutting my eyes to the images rising before me. "I wouldn't."

"Pril. You'll never know how hard this decision has been. I sound resolute and determined but I am so close, I was so close." Her voice broke. "I have come this far alone, but I need someone now. I need . . . someone has to drive me home from the clinic after the . . . after the procedure. Will you do this for me?"

I looked at Ruth, this woman I loved unconditionally and in many ways more deeply than my husband, and thought of need, and women. Need, which motivates women to tend bedraggled, neglected animals and fallen birds; to cultivate barren plots of earth. Need, which drives women to care for and stay with drunks and druggies, sluggers and shouters and bullies. Need, which compels women to give heroic lifetimes to retarded, ruined, deformed, defective children. How ironic that it is women who understand best that "I need you" is a tighter, stronger, more lasting bond than "I love you." *Be-*

119

cause I'm needed is an incentive ultimately stronger than love. "Yes." I nodded. "You know I will."

The strength of Ruth's resolve did not falter; didn't falter as we paid the bill and returned to the inn, Ruth driving still, over the black roadways. Nor did it falter with morning as we dressed, or over our mostly silent breakfast of the best waffles in the state. Ruth ordered nothing.

"Not hungry?" I asked. "Not even coffee?"

"Nothing by mouth for four hours prior," she answered with professional detachment. "D&E requires a local."

Again she drove, checking directions she'd scribbled on the back of a party invitation, its dated, flip-side greetings grotesquely cheerful. "The clinic's only open two days a week," she commented, slowing at a downtown corner. A telephone pole bore a hand-lettered poster: EQUAL RIGHTS FOR UNBORN WOMEN. "Ah," she said, "antiabortion feminists. We must be close." At a squat one-story building Ruth pulled into the parking lot, commenting, "Appropriately anonymous." She noticed my apprehensive glance. "Did you expect picketers?" she asked. Dropping the keys into her shoulder bag, she tapped the steering wheel with her index finger. "Do you want to come inside?"

It was so very very ordinary. So plain, so standard. The potted plant, the sliding window, the registration clipboard, the receptionist in white, the interior door lettered PRIVATE. Ruth was summoned within

minutes of registering, and I was left in the windowless gray-green waiting room. But not left alone. A
half dozen other people aged twenty to fifty, equally
divided between males and females, waited in the
molded plastic seats as well, thumbing ragged magazines listlessly or restlessly, staring at the speckled
linoleum floor. Who were they, and whom had they
brought and how and why had they come to this
end, this decision? What were their reasons? Did
they feel regret or rejoicing, or like Ruth, that un-
emotional resolve? Were they fathers, mothers, sisters, boyfriends, husbands, or like me, a friend? A
scene no different from a thousand other clinics in a
thousand other cities, at clinics for eyes and throats
and stomachs and backs. Clinics for abortions. I
willed myself to think of nothing, and thought only
of Ruth behind the door, alone in the bowels of the
building.

Someone touched my shoulder. "Ready?" I pivoted. Dressed, composed, collected, Ruth handed me
the keys. "Your turn." There was no wheelchair re-
striction, no anesthetic lethargy. She didn't hobble,
or grimace, or take my arm.

She read aloud from a typewritten sheet of pre-
cautions as I drove, ticking them off like a list of Saturday errands. *"'Watch for irregular or heavy
bleeding. For fever. No tampons. Refrain from sexual intercourse one week.'"* She smiled faintly. *"Refrain,"* she repeated. "That won't be too difficult. A
tampon box on the back of the john should do it."

She turned to the window, and I watched her profile. "God, men. They're so squeamish."

We stopped for a red light where a pregnant woman waddled slowly, interminably, across the crosswalk. I drummed my fingers against the wheel, willing the light to flash green.

"Must be in the water," Ruth said. "Bright out, isn't it?"

"Ruth—" I began, helpless in the face of that unnerving composure.

"I didn't get much sleep last night," she interrupted. "Fortunately, taking a nap smack in the middle of the day is standard vacation procedure." She looked my way. "Isn't it?"

At the inn, as Ruth crouched over her bag in search of her nightgown, I tried not to look. Tried not to see the thin elastic belt around her abdomen, the bulk of the pad at her crotch. Tried to ignore the chasm between us. She lay down, and I pulled the rocking chair to the window with a book.

But reading was a futile distraction. My eyes veered every few minutes to Ruth. When a low moan escaped her lips I crossed instantly to the bed and sat down next to her, beside the tender curve of her spine against the vast ocean of bed, her neck frail and vulnerable as a child's. My gut tightened, obliterating any earlier frustration and bafflement with her inexplicable emotionless restraint. She shifted in restless slumber and the nightgown fell from her shoulder, exposing the rounded flesh of a breast, milky white and traced with blue veins. I looked at it, heavy and limp, and thought of nursing: the days of feeding on demand, the nights of swollen, painful engorgement, the mornings when my gown was stiff with dried milk, crackling like a man's starched shirt pocket. Leaning over the sink to brush my teeth, I would smell myself, a whiffed combination of soured milk in school cafeterias and the rich, fetid aroma of sultry greenhouses. I remembered making the bed, spreading the sheet over blotches of leaked milk, like stains of leaking semen, which dripped to the floor weekday mornings as I fixed school lunches. Only receptacles, I thought. Repositories. And there beside my friend, a surge of unreasonable, elemental hatred for men, all men, coursed hotly through me.

She moaned again. "Ruth," I whispered. "I'm here." I stroked her hair. Her eyes twitched beneath the closed lids and she reached for my wrist, stopping its motion. "With Grayson," she said quietly, "I was in labor for ten hours. And I had frosted hair then, so it was coarse and thick. We'd gone to Lamaze classes, you know how you only go to Lamaze that first time, and after that it's strictly drugs. Except for the masochists. The Roslyns." She smiled wanly, and I nodded. "Reed was trying to follow the instructions, to do everything just right. He kept massaging my head, rubbing and rubbing my scalp all those ten hours of tossing and turning my head back and forth on the pillow. When Grayson was finally born, and it was all over, my hair was standing out a foot from my head, greasy and matted and fanned. They gave me a mirror to see myself. Everybody thought it was so funny," she said distantly. "But I never saw the humor in it at all." She turned from me, drawing her knees to her chest in a furled fetal huddle that gripped my heart.

"Can I get you something?"

She laughed, a brittle bark. "Could you get me drunk? I'd like to be drunk." She buried her face in the pillows, and began kneading her belly, wadding the nightgown between her fingers.

"What is it, Ruth?" I asked, alarmed. "Are you in pain? Are you cramping?"

Her answer was whispered. "I was so . . . informed. I went to the library and read the medical books. Asked the questions. Read everything. I know all the correct terms. D&E. Dilatation and evacuation. Uterine cavity. I was so knowledgeable. But they don't tell you, Pril. They don't tell you."

"What?" I leaned close to her face, but her eyes remained squeezed shut.

"And I purposely picked a clinic, not an o.b.'s office. To be with other women. A community. Together. And you *are* together, lying there in a communal recovery room, awake, conscious, but yet not together. Not drugged. Not asleep. But not speaking, not sharing. Like zombies. Because we are cowed and ashamed. Because we hate each other, despise each other for what we have done. Forty-five minutes of recovery!" she spat.

"Ruth, listen to me," I said sternly, afraid. I grasped her upper arms, the muscles rigid and tensed. "They are victims of incest, they have six children, they are pregnant because they were raped, they are twelve and thirteen years old."

"But not me, Pril! Not me!" she cried, a terrible keening wail of mourning. "They don't tell you," she whimpered, and with that bleat of misery something inside me crumbled to dust, and fractured within her as well.

She shuddered, then thrashed away. Convulsive sobs shook her, wracking her body. She curled tighter into herself, knees to chin and fists clenched at her cheeks, and her voice rose with mounting hysteria. "I thought it would be simple, like a pelvic exam. If they had only knocked me out, Pril!"

I grabbed her by the shoulders and forced her face, the features contorted with anguish, close to mine. "Don't, Ruth."

She pulled from my grasp, beyond listening, beyond compassion. "I have to. You have to listen." Her chest heaved with gasping. "I heard it! It sucked, it sucked." She wept, her voice by turns a strangled shout, then tinny with muffled misery. "It's the noise, the sucking, the *evacuation*!" I turned my face aside, as if I might deflect her breakdown, deflect her agony, deflect the harrowing image. "The sucking," she moaned, her arms wrapped across her chest. "You get off the bed, and the stirrups hang there like stocks, like handcuffs, it is like being an animal tied

125

to a post. And you know there is some, some *container* beneath the gurney with a hose leading out of it and your insides and your guts and your baby have traveled inside that clear tubing into that container like soda through a straw, and it will go in a rusted Dumpster and it has taken *ten minutes* and you are empty empty and finished and it has taken only ten minutes!"

I blinked hard and focused on the cheap ceiling acoustical tiles, not Ruth's stricken soliloquy. *Details*, I thought. *Details of the ceiling. Details of the abortion.* Beside me, Ruth groaned and ground the heels of her palms into her eye sockets. "Vital signs!" she croaked. *"Vital signs!"* She began to rock back and forth rhythmically, hypnotically, her hands clasped tightly between her thighs. The mattress shook with her violent trembling. Never never had I witnessed such palpable pain.

I crawled on my knees behind Ruth and pulled her body against my own, curling over her as if I might return her to a womb where there was no guilt, no regret, no choices. "Ssshh," I whispered against her ear, her hair filling my mouth. "I have you, Ruth. I'm here." She grabbed my hands, her fingernails leaving white crescents in my palms. "Stay with me," she said. "Don't leave me." "No, I won't leave you," I said, wanting to give her more than this paltry solace of touch and nearness, but unable to reach that deep, dwarfing grief. We rocked together for long minutes—or hours—until I felt some measure of relaxation, or exhaustion, creep into her tensed limbs. "Lie down," I said, and she did, still crouched into me, still quivering with gulping sorrow.

I held her tightly with wrapped arms and murmured to her and stroked her, and gradually, the sobs subsided to spasmic hiccups. She began to breathe regularly, calmly, until limp and spent and empty, she finally dozed again. Empty of grief, of the child that might have been.

I lit the fire, took the car keys from the dresser, closed the bedroom door, and went into the frigid black night to find an open market. She woke when I returned, and I pulled the blankets and spreads and pillows to the floor around the hearth and wordlessly motioned her beside me. There within the soft nest of linens we cocooned ourselves, huddled and swaddled against the fearsome night, the fearsome truth, with the burgundy glow of fire embers as our only light. We hungrily spooned sliced bananas and sugary milk from water glasses, as if insulated in our warren of quilts and sustained by nursery food, we might return to the uncomplicated chastity of our childhoods.

She was up before me the next morning, dressed but for the worn moccasins she was turning over in her hands. "Look," she said, and held out the shoes. I looked. White adhesive tape striped the length of each inner sole, and on them RUTH CAMPBELL was printed in blocky black letters. Ruth fingered the tapes, an expression of sad wonder on her face. "They did it yesterday," she murmured. "At the clinic. As if I might forget who I was. Like those plastic bracelets our babies wore in the hospital nursery: Baby Girl Campbell. I kept mine." Her face crumpled.

I crossed the room and took the shoes from her. "Tell me how you feel. Are you sore, are you bleeding?"

She shook her head. "No," she said, and touched her chest. "Only here."

I drove. Ruth reclined the seat and stared at the flannelly ceiling of the car. Near the outskirts of Greensboro she finally spoke. "Do you remember how sometimes when we hiked, one of us said something so funny we just fell to the ground and collapsed in hilarity?" The soft tone of her voice had a damaged quality. "We'll never do that again."

"We will!"

She ratcheted up the seat and turned her gaze to me. "No. We'll never take another girls' trip together. This . . . particular journey will always lie in the way, ruining any others. Like scar tissue. The one we remember. It's my fault. I've robbed us both of something. I've killed an innocence as well."

"Oh, Ruth," I contradicted her, "we were never innocent!"

"Yes," she said, "we were."

I switched off the motor in the Campbell driveway. It was still early afternoon, our children at school, our husbands at work. "Thank you," she said, "for coming with me under false pretense, for driving me, for seeing me through that . . . emotional purging."

128

She smiled briefly. "I nearly bought the Stegner book as premature thanks, but the title . . ." She trailed off. "I . . . I couldn't."

I shook my head, unable to speak. We sat for a long intimate, awkward moment, until the heat began to dissipate and the car's interior filled with February's raw chill. Finally I unclasped the seat belt and handed the car keys across the seat to Ruth. Her fingers wrapped around mine in a cold grabbed clutch of desperation.

"Promise me, Pril. Swear. Never. Never, Pril."

I looked into her red-rimmed eyes, seared with grief.

The whites were so strangely fresh, so pure. "No," I said simply. "Never."

"Mrs. Henderson, do you know of any reason, or any circumstance, or any situation that may have precipitated Mrs. Campbell's decision?" The attorney looked at the ceiling as I had two years earlier, stalling. "Some motivation for her departure?"

"Motivation." *The word caught and held me.* "Narrative is easy," *I'd said;* "it's the motivation that is so difficult." *"Do you always have to have a reason, Pril?" Ruth had said.*

"Mrs. Henderson?"

I lifted my gaze, and Ruth filled it, her expression devoid of pleading, or fear of exposure, or hope for mercy. The child would be nearly two now. Walking. Talking.

"No," I said. "Never."

"Never?" the attorney echoed, a question implicit in his tone. The court reporter looked up expectantly.

"None," I corrected myself. "No reason."

Chapter 9

A week after Ruth and I returned from the mountains, Berk returned also; came home to the white house on the hill. He arrived with neither advance notice nor fanfare. But for his jeep in the driveway we might never have known, so immersed, presumably, were the reunited couple in themselves. I can picture him humbly begging forgiveness, sheepishly requesting to be received into the bosom of his home and family. Or the bosom of his wife. I can picture Roslyn relenting as well, as Berk cunningly wooed and cooed his deceitful way back into her heart, and home, and bed.

He proved himself a worthy actor in a charade, playing the part of contrite remorseful husband come to his senses. He probably chatted about moving back in, the bothersome logistics of breaking his apartment lease, disconnecting the phone, combining his checking account with hers. No doubt they discussed future plans, vowed to change behavior, expectations, attitudes. On the seventh day Roslyn waved him away, blithely euphoric, sated with rediscovered security, and sex. Taking a walk that afternoon, Ruth and I saw her for the first time in a week. She slowed the car to speak, unable to suppress the grin stretching across her cheeks.

"Berk's back," she said.

"We noticed," Ruth said.

"I'm so glad," I put in. "Happy?" Roslyn blushed and nodded. "Want to walk with us? We'll go round the block and meet you at your house."

"Can't, thanks. I'm on my way to the gynecologist."

"Something wrong?" Ruth asked.

Roslyn giggled girlishly and shook her head. "Just cystitis. You know, the 'honeymoon disease.' " Beside me, Ruth purposely stepped on the heel of my sneaker. For all of the carnal conversations between Ruth and me, we both inwardly cringed for Roslyn and her coy revelation.

But at nightfall Berk didn't return. He had stayed one week. Seven short days, but long enough.

"Don't," Ruth had advised. *"Don't get a job. Don't be capable."*

"Don't," I'd said. *"Don't give up."*

"Don't sign anything," we'd warned.

"Don't despair. Don't forgive. Don't hold out hopes."

Don't. Don't. Don't. Don't let him move back in the house. Change the locks. Don't sleep with him, we should have said, as innocent as Roslyn of Berk's calculated act of destruction; naively unaware that sleeping with a separated spouse is viewed by the court as an act of forgiveness. Even a night on a sofa in a house from which one spouse has left or abandoned legally effectively erases all claims of adultery, negating any suit for damages by the formerly injured party. And Berk had managed much more than merely spending the night. In the face of his false affections and persuasions of sincerity, what little guard Roslyn possessed dropped away easily as her clothes. Apparently there was no limit to Berk's capacity for destruction, and no limit to Roslyn's capacity for trust.

Three days later, a new package of papers arrived. Official notices of division of goods, dates and times slated for appraisal of jointly owned property—furniture, silver, even the dishes in the cabinets and the paintings on the walls. "Miscellaneous Glassware in Kitchen" Berk valued at forty dollars, and twenty-five was assigned to "Children's Halloween Costumes in Living Room Chest." Instructed by his lawyer, Berk had videotaped the contents of the entire house—every drawer, closet, cupboard, and shelf—to counterbalance and offset his salary, stocks, retirement fund, his every financial holding, so that a judge might deem that miscellaneous glassware and Halloween costumes added up to assets aplenty, enough to sustain Roslyn financially without tapping too deeply into his earned income. As if she had ever protested. The house was to be appraised and sold immediately, the proceeds divided. Within forty-eight hours a metal FOR SALE sign was bluntly hammered into the frozen front yard. The treachery and the severance were finished. A complete division of goods, and history, and lives.

One hears of "insults to the brain," implying terrible physical trauma—accidents, falls, beatings, and bludgeonings—but Roslyn's mind, her fragile psyche, was no less affected or assaulted. She was beyond comprehension, beyond anger, deep in some murky netherworld of shock and misery that dimmed and blotted Berk's cowardly, calculated atrocity. In a stupefaction of suffering she stood dazedly by, a silent zombie as appraisers and bankers and real estate agents with strange couples in tow tested windows and toilets, gauged closet space and dishwater longevity. She didn't seek us out. She retreated within her house and herself, a hollow-eyed victim. I saw her only once, so reclusive was she, but I knew those vacant, friendless eyes. I'd seen a younger, lesser version of them three decades earlier in Poor Polly Franklin's face at Kiahwassee. I should have recognized that radiating pain and acted, intervened. We both should have, Ruth and I. "He had a chance to be a hero," Roslyn had once joked about Berk when hunting cohorts had canceled a scheduled weekend trip. Berk had gone anyway, alone, when he might have stayed home with Roslyn. He could have been a hero.

There was something ghoulish and predestined about the funereal flow of expensive vehicles hopeful real estate agents piloted by the Lawrence house. "I hope it's not more old people," Beth said as we watched another sleek Mercedes make its lingering pace up the opposite street. I let the remark pass, knowing it represented Beth's—and all the children's—anger at circumstances and events their parents could neither control nor fix. The inevitable sale of the house saddened them; invited or uninvited, they had crossed the Lawrence threshold many more times than we adults. In the aromatic recesses of the cedar closets they had played Monster and Sardines, eaten thick slabs of French toast on Saturday mornings in the kitchen. They had cozied deep in Berk's leather armchairs in the den, and stood at the base of his glass-fronted gun cabinet admiring the dully gleaming wood stocks and metal fittings. But by far they loved best the multipaned sleeping porch upstairs, a quaint architectural oddity with three walls of windows—thirty-six, Sloan had proudly announced. The sleeping porch was a ready-made yard sale, cluttered with intriguing outgrown toys—spy attaché cases, an electric football game whose rigid plastic players rattled across the dented tin playing field, stacks of *National Geographic*s, an old cot whose mattress the children upended as a makeshift sliding board. A room for cast-offs.

On a Tuesday afternoon Jay went in search of those *National Geographics*, hoping that their photographs would compensate for the lack of research he'd done on a social studies term project. The incident a decade earlier, when Roslyn found Jay wandering unsupervised about her yard, was an ironic prophecy. This time it was Jay who found Roslyn.

Eyes closed, she lay peacefully on the sleeping porch cot, and, as he had ten years earlier with the bird, Jay believed she was only sleeping. But like the bird, she wasn't sleeping; thick, glistening blood pooled beneath her head on the mattress ticking. Not sleeping, but shot through the skull with a single, self-inflicted suicidal bullet from her husband's own convenient, accessible arsenal of weapons.

"She's harmless," Ruth had said of Roslyn. Harmless. Poor wronged Roslyn, harmless to everyone but herself.

Questions from the police and attending physician were pointed and peppered as buckshot, despite the undertones of solicitous consolation. I seemed to watch from above, as though a dress rehearsal were being enacted, a scene I'd composed at the typewriter: Ruth and me in jeans and limp turtlenecks whose cuff elastic had long before succumbed to laundered exhaustion, opposite nattily uniformed figures of authority nonetheless too late to assist, all united in Roslyn's sparkling, American-made kitchen. I answered with rote monosyllables, incapable and unwilling to condense events of six months into a one-line blank on a computer-generated form. Ruth wasn't better, only more belligerent. "Did you have any idea?" "No," I said. "What do you think?" Ruth asked indignantly. "It's standard, ma'am," the officer said gently. "Was there any kind of note or letter?" "No." "Had you seen her recently?" "No," I said. "Define recently," Ruth said. "Had she ever demonstrated any indications or symptoms she might harm herself? To take her life?" "Such as what?" Ruth asked. "Well,"—the officer hesitated uncomfortably—"self-destructive impulses?" "Of course not," Ruth said. "She was a Pied Piper Superwife who hit the glass ceiling." "Pardon?" the officer asked. Ruth gave the officer a minimal glance. "You'll have to ask her husband for more details."

Took her life. I was silent, suddenly focused by the archaic gentility of the phrase, a euphemism of my parents' generation. Details materialized, details that surely would be considered Not Applicable on any dotted line. Of Roslyn's incredibly, unnaturally even teeth, the dentured conformity I'd once admired aloud to her. "Oh yes," she'd said. "My Chiclet choppers. I grind them at night. Unconsciously. By the time I'm sixty they'll be filed down to pure gums." I remembered the stiff fibrous cuticle she'd ripped away so casually as she talked to us, how she'd ignored the pain, the half moon of blood springing round the nail. My gaze fell on a reminder note Roslyn had affixed to the refrigerator with a perky Oreo cookie magnet. *"Amaryllis in dark closet Nov.*

29," it read. So she would know when to bring the fat bulb into the sunshine, to a warm undisturbed corner where the flower could open its blazing, glorious trumpet safe from lethal cold. *That,* I wanted to say, *that note is a self-destructive impulse.* Such a passion for detail cannot have been easy to live with. Ruth had answered curtly for both of us.

"Took her life." Not a phrase that appeared on any of the dog-eared pages of the library book Ruth showed me later. How like Ruth to seek out information, to look for validation of the senseless in the graphs and charts and columns of statistics. Factual, irrefutable information illustrating how by 1980, among women, "pacific" and "passive" means of suicide—pills, carbon monoxide, other poisons—yielded to firearms as the "preferred" method, *"'particularly in the American South,'"* Ruth read. The only information omitted was a physical description of Roslyn, for everything else, all other reasons, were described and detailed in lengthy, scholarly text. "Those women who kill themselves after a man deserts them do so because they can no longer fill their social functions as mothers and wives. The highest suicide rates among women are found among those who are most submerged in the family." The facts and findings and analyses culminated in one harsh, elementary conclusion: Men most often commit suicide because of financial strain or depression. Women kill themselves because of men.

Accident, suicide, or natural causes, the requirements of death move forward inexorably as an assembly line. Thrust into circumstances they were ill-equipped to confront, William, Trey, and David were numbly stoic, moving robotically through the rituals of receiving, waiting, public grieving. Scotty and Reed paced the porch, uncomfortable with the language of loss, nervously jingling the change in their pants pockets and making conversation with strangers. For two days Ruth and I were part of the backdrop of death, taking stance at the Lawrence door, in the kitchen. The number of women who came to the house laden with their helpless offerings of sympathy—food—astonished me. I didn't know the names or faces of these fringe friends. I arranged and served and wrapped, ashamed at my unwitting arrogance, my presumption that Ruth and I were close to Roslyn, when we in fact lay squarely among the ranks of those secondary acquaintances.

With survivor's guilt, I told myself that Ruth and I didn't purposely exclude Roslyn. She had always been beyond Ruth and me, beyond the stage of life when we were linked by Legos and small-scale penury and half-decorated houses and sugar-cube igloos for social studies projects. Roslyn had more money, more children, more time.

And this is true, though it is also true that Roslyn Lawrence was ultrafeminine and submissive, and Ruth and I wanted no contamination by or connection to those traits. Had we only reached out earlier perhaps, tried harder, allowed Roslyn some degree of the special relationship we shared, I might not have been left wondering, agonizing how I might have intervened and prevented Roslyn's tragedy, prevented my son his grisly discovery. I was too late for Roslyn, too late to shield my son.

Berk didn't come to the funeral. Thus Ruth and I attended to the details. Because after the mourners and ministers have departed, after the food is frozen and the prayers have ceased, women are left to pick up the pieces and tend to the details. Then, again, and always. No one noticed the trickled stains of rusty-colored blood that had silently leaked from the second floor, ruining those fine plaster walls at the kitchen ceiling. But Ruth and I did. We removed the dusty, decorative collection of baskets above the cabinet containing "forty dollars of miscellaneous glassware," and scoured those walls. We rolled up the thin cot pallet and took it to a Dumpster miles away. We threw away the magazines, the board games, a broken iron, shredded silk lampshades. We gave away books and clothes, costume jewelry and a battered box of peau-de-soie bridesmaid pumps.

We didn't look for a note, nor did we find one. "No," Ruth said. "Ninety percent of suicides don't leave notes. Only the ones who want to be stopped." We righted overturned ladderback chairs and cleared off the braided scatter rug and dragged the vacuum cleaner into the sleeping porch and located an outlet. The machine chewed and whirred obligingly, and in its whined electric suck we smelled the pungent tang of pine, refreshing as spring, woodsy as winter. And because we were wives and mothers and caretakers we knew that what we smelled were needles of a Christmas tree, dried and embedded in the appliance's black canister interior, emitting an aroma that in other circumstances might have been rich with pleasant remembrance. The scent of Fraser fir needles Roslyn had not so long ago dutifully vacuumed herself.

*C*hapter 10

W*hen was the last time you saw the defendant?"*
"The afternoon before she left to go skiing."
"And, Mrs. Henderson, would you categorize this ski trip as a last-minute, impromptu vacation decision, or a calculated, long-range, long-planned exit?"
"I don't know."

I still don't.

Examined and remembered, everything about that final twenty-four hours seems freighted with portent, laden with omen. Every gesture, statement, phrase, and smile, every touch. An ordinary day, our last.

I stood in the doorway of the Campbells' toolshed, only partially joking as I asked, "How dare you leave me alone and defenseless for ten entire days?" Ruth foraged in a rear corner crowded with tomato stakes, lacrosse sticks, and a bicycle pump.

It was Good Friday afternoon, the children freshly freed from the bondage of formal education. The next morning Ruth was leaving with Sloan and Grayson to go skiing for the entire spring break. The impromptu trip had materialized soon after Roslyn's funeral. Ruth was taking them West, to one of the big-time, big-name, big-mountain resorts—Aspen, Vail, Jackson Hole, Telluride. I wasn't certain of her exact destination and wasn't even particularly interested. I knew only that she was going, and that I would miss her.

"You'll have Reed," Ruth said, her voice muffled by stacks of clay pots and burlap leaf bags. "If you can crowbar him away from the television." Reed wasn't going; the trip had been too hastily organized for him to cancel commitments at work.

Easter came early that year, in late March, as had warmer weather in general. College basketball playoffs were in full swing, marching inexorably to the national titles and championships that annually paralyze North Carolinians. Evenings, meals, and work schedules were dictated by game times of the state's high-ranked college teams, exacting a slowing of everyday pace, yet quickening of an adrenaline sports pulse I was never prepared for. While Ruth rummaged I tried to imagine falling flakes, ice-skating rinks, a snow-covered landscape, and failed. "Are you sure there'll be snow?"

"Winter lasts at least another month out there. It's the latitude."

"Altitude," I corrected. "I still think you're brave, or crazy, taking on the Rocky Mountains, black diamond slopes, and two kids—alone."

Something clattered ominously in the depths of the shadowed shed. "Found it," Ruth announced triumphantly, extracting a plastic bottle of fungicide from the clutter. "I knew it was in here somewhere." In her other hand she held a white paper bag aloft. "Right under the narcissus bulbs I meant to force." She squeezed the bag and grimaced. "So rotten they feel like sponges." She looked across the lawn mower that separated us, thinking my thoughts. *Amaryllis in dark closet Nov. 29.* Roslyn had been dead three weeks. "How is Jay?" she asked quietly.

"I honestly don't know. Quiet and reserved. Absorbed. I'm trying to get him to talk about it. He seems more sad than anything, and surely that's normal."

"Children have cores and reserves of strength adults know nothing of. They're more resilient than you imagine. We grown-ups don't give them the credit they deserve for withstanding crises. War, famine. Suicide."

"I hope so."

"I know so." She stepped delicately backward again, avoiding a large latticed grill Reed had had specially welded for a one-time backyard oyster roast. "Here," she said, stretching and handing the fungicide to me. "Now don't lose it. Your toolshed looks like the Black Hole of Calcutta." Behind the screen was a tangle of metal supports, concentric circles soldered to three right-angle prongs. She jerked them upward, releasing them from the grid, and lunged over a redwood planter toward the door and me.

We walked across her yard to the back border. Fluorescent plastic Easter eggs dangled by strings from the lower branches of a spindly dogwood in the adjacent yard. I pointed and said, "Please explain that tradition to me." Ruth laughed.

Beneath the neighbor's tree, the slender silvery foliage of early spring jonquils come and gone was neatly folded and knotted. "Look at those poor things," I went on. "Bound and tied like Chinese feet." I looked over Ruth's border, its casual, artful combination of evergreens behind deciduous shrubs, which, their sap quickened, were making tentative forays toward flowering.

Ruth shook her head sadly. "I wish something had been blooming in our yards for Roslyn's grave."

I nodded, agreeing. We'd visited the cemetery on the way to the Maundy Thursday evening service. Surprisingly, Ruth had called me to go to church with her. "I'm not too religious about religion," she always claimed. "But I should take the children—give them something to rebel against."

The mystery, liturgy, and tradition of my faith propelled me to services. Habit more than desire. But despite her protests, Ruth knew more of religion and theology—interpretation, history, conflicting beliefs and versions—than anyone I'd ever met. Whenever I came across an obscure biblical reference in my reading, I had only to ask Ruth where to locate it in the Bible, and what it meant. She could explain synoptic Gospels, various meanings of love in Greek, the lineages of Sarah and Rebecca and women I'd never heard of, but she steadfastly eschewed attending church. Scotty and I had argued one night about her stance of refusal; whether full, true faith could be realized in solitude, or whether the nurture of community was necessary. I'd wished for Ruth as Scotty refuted every reasoning and justification I invented. She could have flattened his defenses like a steamroller.

Though it was real enough, the store-bought Easter lily had looked stupidly, splendidly fake beside the simple marble marker of Roslyn's grave. Ruth had stripped away the foil wrapping, hardly improving on the plastic container. As I wedged the pot back and forth into the still-raw red clay to better secure it, the pointed symmetrical leaves jutting from the stem bobbed briefly over the succinct engraving of name and dates, then listed drunkenly to the right. "God," I said. "That lily is so, I don't know, *generic*."

"I know," Ruth said. "But it's the reason behind the gesture that matters." She eyed me mischievously. "You know, Pril, the *motivation*. Never mind," she said. "Someone will steal it before Sunday anyway."

"What?" Such sacrilegious larceny had never occurred to me.

"Happens all the time. Unless cemetery habits have improved since I used to go with my mother to put flowers on my father's grave. Some stranger takes it to their own beloved's headstone." She laughed shortly. "As if God doesn't know." We stood another moment in the gathering darkness, killing time before the service began. "My mother makes three wreaths every Christmas," Ruth said. "Two for our double front doors, and one for my father's grave. The job takes her nearly all day. Reed has always thought it the most wonderful gesture. I've warned him not to die and expect me to make wreaths for his grave." I laughed. "Would you do it for Scotty?"

"No," I assured her.

"Do you ever think . . ." Ruth began.

"What?"

"Sometimes when Reed and I fight, he's asked, 'Do you really love me, Ruth?' And it seems like such a huge question. Terrible, one of those that makes you want to cross yourself superstitiously, like now that it's been mentioned it might come true. But the truth is, sometimes I look at him and think, *Do I?* And it scares me."

"The question, or the answer?"

"Both." If she wanted my answer, she didn't wait for it. Ruth checked her watch. "Time to go." My answer would have been, yes, I wonder sometimes if I love him.

147

Susan S. Kelly

I couldn't recall the last time I'd been to an evening church service. The tone was hushed, muted as the stained glass windows lacking daylight to illuminate their colors. I'd heard the words, the prayers, the psalm many times, but that night, minus the Sunday morning rustles of children whispering their boredom, golfers shifting impatiently during sermons that threatened their tee-times, the words held a deeper, more meaningful reverence, tension, and significance. At the last chord of the recessional I turned to gather my purse from the pew, but Ruth placed her hand over mine, stopping me.

The two priests and acolytes moved about the sacristy and altar, their movements smooth, fluid, unrushed. Taking no notice of one another, each performed his prescribed duty: extinguishing the candles, folding the altar cloths, sliding communion cushions to one side, closing the gate. The brass cross above the altar, the carved wooden crucifix behind the lectern were likewise slowly, solemnly undraped of their gauzy purple Lenten veils and stowed away. Finally the ministers and their young assistants removed their own vestments, richly embroidered or plain white for the acolytes. The altar and its officiants were pared and pruned and humbled of all material trappings. Every action was undertaken in utter, tomblike silence, and with the participants' final genuflection, the overhead lighting was extinguished, casting the nave in abrupt dramatic darkness. The blunt, hushed solemnity of the symbolic service, the stripping of the

148

altar, pricked tears behind my eyelids. Beside me, Ruth had watched the proceedings with calm countenance and serene expectation.

Now, a few hours before her flight, Ruth stood in her garden and fingered the pliable leaves of a knee-high deutzia shrub, soft as eiderdown. Its flowers, the tiny profusion of white blossoms lushly delicate as a bridal veil, were still safely encased in tight cocoons of green. "I'll miss this," she said.

"You won't miss it. Deutzia's always late. By the time you come back the spirea should be blooming too." My voice belied the apprehension I felt for the tender sprouts, coaxed and tempted into timid exposure by temporary, counterfeit warmth. I feared for their presumptuousness, for a vengeful freeze certain to come. For all our fabled Southern clime, late March snowstorms weren't unusual. "I could never be a farmer. Even a thunderstorm breaks the stems, breaks your heart. So much potential for disaster beyond your control."

Pursing her lips at my comment or at the task before her, Ruth knelt, combing her hair away from her brow with her fingers. Thin streaks of gray were visible, wiry strands against the dark brown. I watched her shoulder grow taut with the effort of muscling the supports into the ground. At forty-four Ruth was still strikingly beautiful, model willowy yet enviously firm and supple, thanks no doubt to the riding, a sport I'd never considered exercise. All writing had given me was a permanent furrowed crease between my eyebrows that resisted concealing makeup. "Will you ride out there?" I asked.

"Remember the woman in the Sundance catalog? I'll ride all the time." *Then,* I've thought. Her only slip. But the reference to the catalog Ruth had shown me so long ago diverted my attention, and diminished what she said next as well. "What will you do?"

I assumed she was asking me how I would fill the coming week. Not how I would fill the future. "Learn how to use my new toy." A first-prize short story award included five hundred dollars, which I'd combined with a savings stash to purchase a computer. "When you come home I'll be a computer geek. It ought to save me incredible time on my writing."

"Do you think that will do it?"

"Do what?"

Over her shoulder she gave me an assessing stare. "How's the book going?"

"Let's not discuss it. Ask me when you get back."

Ruth moved to the next plants, struggling to evenly space the prongs just outside the stems. Peonies, results of a winter's worth of debate and research over the merits of peonies versus roses.

"This is a no-brainer, Ruth," I'd declared as we perused the magazines and catalogs that arrived with January to torment us with their horticultural perfection. "Would you rather have that unequivocal, unparalleled, I'll grant you, show-stopping splendor of peonies for three weeks out of the entire year, or have beautiful roses from April through maybe even

Thanksgiving? How is that even a decision? No contest."

"Eureka!" Ruth exclaimed as answer. We were drinking coffee in front of a fire at my house, our children "doing their gender things" as Ruth put it, the girls making snow cream in the kitchen, the boys pelting each other with snowballs outside. "This picture of asters—'a must for every perennial border. Needs no staking,'" she quoted, "is the identical picture to this one!" she crowed, holding up two different catalogs. "It's a hoax. A conspiracy to make us buy." She flipped the page. "I'm getting peonies."

I was mystified by her decision. "But roses give you more of everything! More blossoms, longer blooming season."

"But roses have to have much more attention. They need spraying and fertilizing and pruning."

"Okay, so?"

"They *need* too much of everything. Devotion. Diligence, time, attention, caring, love."

I couldn't argue; it was true. And in the end, she had ordered the peonies—"pennies," Sloan had always insisted on mispronouncing them—and I had ordered roses. A simple case of choice.

I toed a scuffed patch of earth. With a city park across the street, our yards had been spared swing sets, but the wooden disc of a homemade swing had hung for years from a thick branch twenty feet above us. The swing was gone, but the ground beneath it remained scoured and barren, too densely packed by scraping feet of children to ever grow grass again. "I'll be thinking of you during Easter lunch, imagining you on the slopes or sipping hot chocolate in some après-ski lounge. While we're eating lamb and mint jelly," I said. Ruth said nothing so I prattled on. "I hate lamb. I've always hated it despite the fact that it's supposed to be some wonderful seasonal delicacy. It leaves a film on the roof of your mouth, like one of those lift-off magic slate things the children used to get for favors at birthday parties." We hadn't even dyed eggs yet. Still Ruth said nothing. "You might have invited us to go with you," I added with mock petulance.

Ruth stood and faced me. "Would you have come?"

"No," I said ruefully and truthfully. We couldn't have gone. Wouldn't have gone. Too much money, too short a notice. "Don't mind me. I'm just suffering from greener-grass syndrome."

Ruth nodded, understanding. "Have you ever wanted something so badly you think you'll go crazy?"

I cocked my head, and smiled.

"What?" Ruth asked.

"When I was about thirteen, I asked my father how you knew if you loved someone enough to marry them. He told me that when you loved someone so much that it was hard to breathe, or think, or sleep every minute you were apart from them, then you know. I guess that applies as wanting something so badly you think you'll go crazy. I remember feeling that way, crazy for Scotty. Don't you?"

Licking her lips, Ruth looked away at the gaudy dangling Easter eggs. "Ah, you and your blasted memory," she said with feigned disgust.

I quoted some forgotten source. " 'The capital of a writer.' "

"But since then," she pressed. "Haven't you wanted anything? Some yearning so intense that you'd do anything to satisfy it if only you could figure out what it is you wanted?"

I heard her beseeching question, and remembered a casual statement Scotty had made about Ruth years earlier: "Ruth seems to be searching for something. Maybe the feminist cause is it." I'd thought his comments faintly patronizing, and told him so. Now, it seemed the beseeching in her words and tone was nearly palpable. "Yes," I said. "There is something."

"What?"

I looked at Ruth, shrugged. Our intimacy was such that my confession held no shame, no embarrassment at its naked truthfulness. "I've never intended to be exceptional. I just want someone to say I have promise."

"Oh, Pril," Ruth said. She took my hand, twirled my wedding ring. "Does it have to be someone else? Do you need someone else's affirmation? Isn't it enough that *you* believe you have promise?" She kicked at a violet encroaching on a peony's territory.

"I guess not," I admitted.

Ruth grunted as she speared the final cage around the last peony. "Finished," she said, standing back. When the plants were fully branched, the supports would be invisible. She clasped her hipbones. "Do you know what the hardest thing about a peony is?"

"Hardest?" I asked, puzzled.

"Deciding every year whether to cut and put them in a vase indoors, or just look at them, enjoy them outside. Does that sound crazy? Naomi's stablehand, Jerry, grows peonies; four dozen bushes in a twenty-by-twenty plot. And you know what? The decision never torments him. He has absolutely no interest in cutting them. He grows peonies simply to look at them massed in the garden." She held her palms upward in querying, defeated gesture. "Why can't I be like that, happy with just looking at them where they grow?"

"Maybe it's a man thing, the pride in producing," I suggested playfully, waiting for her to take the bait, but she didn't. "Can't you do both? Have them inside and outside?"

"Yes," she said softly. "I guess it's a man thing."

Sorrow fringed her tone, a pall of heaviness I couldn't pierce. I tried again. "You used to bring them into the house. All the time."

"They get all blowsy and overblown and sad and pathetic sitting in a vase."

"I remember when you said peonies past their prime smelled like sex," I said. She glanced swiftly at me. "Oh, Ruth," I said, struck by the apparent seriousness of her quandary. "They get overblown and pathetic on the plant too."

She touched a bud tiny as an English pea, still tightly encased in green, burgundy-edged triangles. "Actually, this is what I like the best. Even more than the blooms. The promise." Her fingers moved over the bushes, silently counting. "Thirty-eight buds this year. After four years I'm finally seeing a payoff." I understood that, comprehended what Ruth meant: the sheer, lovely possibility contained in those simple spheres of buds. In another month they would be fat as marbles.

"You were right about peonies," Ruth said suddenly. "They're so brief before they're gone. But, God, they are beautiful, aren't they? The ruffled petals. The fullness. Whiter than chalk. Or pink, pink as, as . . . Easter." She passed her hand over her eyes. "Remember Roslyn's Easter party for Bethie and Sloan?"

I remembered. Who could forget such perfection planned and carried out entirely for the benefit of two unappreciative five-year-olds and four of their friends? Roslyn had rented a long table and covered it with crisp white embroidered tablecloth, set with sterling forks and teaspoons and bone china. In the center of the table a topiary rabbit held a silver basket of beautifully decorated eggs Roslyn had pierced, blown hollow, and painstakingly marbled with paintbrushes and sponges. Satin bows swagged from the tiered cake stand, adorned the neck of the ivied bunny, and twined among the woven silver handles of tiny baskets. Every detail of the party had been pale and pastel: butter mints and Jordan almonds in fluted paper holders, lime and raspberry sherbet, yellow sponge cake frosted with pink. For favors each child had received a coveted treasure of my own youth: an oversized egg prickly with encrystalled sugar and a ribbon of hardened pink icing encircling a peephole. Within the egg lay a three-dimensional view, a pastoral spring diorama of eggs hidden among flowers and grass. The girls were enchanted with the miniature tableau so finely detailed, so beautifully captured. They were for keeping, those eggs, not eating. But where are those eggs now, their pretty perfection? Boxed in the attic, the sugared crust carbonized by heat, alongside hard waxy puddles of melted Christmas candles. Symbols all, details. Like Palm Sunday crosses forgotten and collecting in a kitchen drawer; dry and stiff and fragile as husks, threatening to disintegrate with every probe for screws, rubber bands, matches.

Inspired by the remembrance of the eggs, the magazine, I suddenly placed Ruth's earlier reference. "The Sundance catalog!" I exclaimed. "Oh, Ruth, this summer, let's live a catalog life. Let's have outdoor suppers with torches and watermelon centerpieces and drinks in wheelbarrows full of ice, and citronella candles and canvas umbrellas. Nasturtium blossom salads. Let's," I implored.

Ruth looked at me tenderly, indulgently. "I can't

even manage to force bulbs, Pril. Besides, don't you remember? Those pictures. It's all a hoax."

Behind us a storm window slammed. We turned. "Mom!" Sloan bellowed from the open upstairs window. "I can't find the gloves I got for Christmas, and I need to pack them!"

"Be right there!" Ruth called, and touched the buds crowning the stalks again. "There's a theory that when peonies begin blooming you should cut off all these outside ones, the weaklings, so the plant's energy goes into producing one huge, bigger, stronger bloom. But you have to decide that too!" she cried, a peculiarly plaintive desperation to her voice. "You have to decide whether to sacrifice smaller blooms for a bigger one. It's a choice."

She touched my arm as we walked toward the house. "Listen, Pril, there's something else," she said hurriedly. "Peonies don't transplant well."

I looked at her, the small nails against my freckled forearm. She stroked her throat nervously, then laughed feebly. "What am I doing? Obsessing about flowers, for God's sake. You probably think I'm crazy." She brushed her hair from her forehead again.

"You're doing the Robert Redford farewell thing," I said. Ruth caught herself, dropped her hand, and smiled her beautiful wide smile at me. "Don't worry," I said. "I'll look after my roses. And your peonies. And Reed. We'll have him over for the basketball finals."

"Reed . . ." she repeated distractedly.

"What time does your plane leave again?"
"Eight ten."
"Want me to take you to the airport?"
She shook her head. "Reed is."
"Okay, then. Have a great time."
Ruth flipped her hand. "Bye."
"See you when you get back," I said, the ordinary farewell of any friend.

But she never came back. And I was not just any friend.

$\mathscr{C}$ hapter 11

I heard from Ruth in only two days, a postcard she'd mailed from the Denver airport. In the small square of space she'd scrawled, *"The stewardess whispered to me that I had a stain on my jeans (white jeans, of course!). I thought I'd dropped some of the lunch lasagna. Silly me. Knew you'd want to know. Love, Ruth."* I had laughed long and hard before dropping the card in the pile of papers next to my computer. I have it still.

To Reed she wrote a letter. Before it arrived, though, not one but two nights of hard freezes transformed the promising green buds of the peonies into shriveled marbles scorched black with cold. I never knew the actual contents of her letter, but it had the same stunting, killing effect. Ruth followed the advice she had given to me. Only she was silent and cunning. I was exiled.

Scotty looked up from the stack of saltine crackers he routinely devoured every evening before dinner as Reed flung open our back door. But Reed ignored Scotty. He strode over to me and shoved an envelope under my nose. Though his hands shook, I could see Ruth's handwriting. "Did you know?" he demanded. Confused, I reached for the letter, but he jerked it back, slapping it against his palm with a sharp smack. "Did you know?" he thundered. "You knew!"

"Take it easy, Reed," Scotty said. "What's going on?"

Reed slitted his eyes, glaring at me. "Ask her." His mouth was set thin as a blade. "Go ahead, Pril. Tell him. You obviously didn't plan to tell *me*."

Alarmed, I said, "What are you talking about? Is it Ruth? The children?" Visions of avalanches, broken limbs, frostbite flashed before me.

Reed fairly spat. "It's Ruth, all right." He nodded, inanely continuing to bob his head while he formed the words. "She's fine. She's so fine, in fact, that she's staying on."

"Longer?" I asked. "What about school starting?"

"Longer than '*longer*,'" Reed growled. "*Permanently.*"

"Come on, Reed," Scotty said. "Those are standard vacation lines. As in, wish you were here, having such a wonderful time we're never coming home, et cetera," Scotty went on, blithe and comic, but Reed bored his eyes into me. My legs felt spongy and slack.

Without asking, without clarification, I knew there was no mistake. But I knew because I knew Ruth. Not because she had told me.

"No, Scotty," Reed said. He rubbed his thumb across the handwritten address, Ruth's own address. "She's very precise about her . . . intentions. Ruth is not coming back. Not tomorrow, as scheduled, or next week, or ever." He turned on me again. "Tell us all about it, Pril. You and Ruth are thicker than thieves."

My mind clicked with a thousand conversations clamoring to be reheard. "Why?" I whispered.

"*Why?*" Reed parroted. "You tell me why. It's not like she sent me an itemized list of reasons," he said, and slapped the letter against the table. "Some feminist bullshit."

I sat down heavily in one of the chairs before the table set for supper. "I didn't know, Reed. I didn't." Ruth, I thought wildly. Not coming home. Never coming back to Reed, or her house, or me. How could she?

Reed walked to the window, crossed his arms high at the sash, and buried his head between them. "Please tell me what about our life, what about me, is so heinous that Ruth would . . . abandon it." From the television in the adjoining room the crowd roared its approval of a three-point shot. "Eighteen years," he murmured, "eighteen years concludes with my wife driving off into the sunset because she, she . . ."—he glanced at the letter again—"because

161

she wants, pardon me, *needs* to start over. *Start over?*" His voice rose with incredulity. "If it weren't so clichéd it'd be hilarious. *Thelma and Louise* stuff." Anger flushed his face again. "Except that I haven't done anything to deserve it, as you goddamn well know."

I watched his pain, the swift changes from fury to wounding and perplexity. "Oh, he *adores* her," Roslyn had said of Reed and Ruth, and years later the same zip of envy surged through me. "Maybe it's not about you, Reed," I offered softly. "Maybe it's about her."

Scotty curled his lip with plain disdain for my explanation. I read his expression: If you can't say something helpful, shut up. Ever the voice of reason, he spoke. "Wait a minute, Reed. You're upset, and no wonder. But you've exaggerated the situation. Give Ruth a little time. This is awfully sudden, and for no apparent reason. I know it sounds lame, but maybe Ruth has just been swept up in that whole resort atmosphere. That Western allure."

"I'll tell you what I'm not going to do," Reed said. "I'm not going to just sit here and take it. Like . . ." his voice fell off, ". . . like Roslyn. It's desertion and kidnapping to boot. Like the soap operas and talk shows and all that media shit. Ruth has kidnapped the children. Apparently she thinks I'll just take this lying down, but she has another think coming, the . . ." I waited for the final word, "bitch," but he stopped. His next words were pathetic with yearning and agony. "I will not let her go so easily, do you understand?" He spoke directly to me, then left as quickly as he'd come. Though Reed didn't see it, I nodded. He loved Ruth. I understood; I loved her too.

Suddenly overcome with exhaustion, I rested my chin on my folded knee and rubbed my forehead, kneading the brows, the furrowed skin. Misinterpreting the gesture as one of relief, Scotty looked piercingly at me. "Well. *Did* you know?"

My head snapped up. Had I had the strength, I would have lunged at him. "If I was going to lie, Scotty, don't you think I'd lie as easily to you as to Reed?" The implications of my question stopped him cold, foreshadowing scenes between us yet to come. Scotty walked into the den, joining the children and the basketball game, leaving me alone with my own questions; questions only one person could answer. How *could* you? How could you *leave*? How could you leave *me*?

There is something agonizing about waiting for letters or calls that do not come; agonizing at first and then deadening. I should have been accustomed to it, God knows. But all my previous waits had been for letters or calls from strangers, faceless editors. Not Ruth. Two weeks became a month, then six weeks, then two months with no missive, no message. No explanation or apology, no change of heart or mind or intent, no word. Even the children received letters from Sloan and Grayson: Bethie's envelope drooled with hardened purple sealing wax, Jay's *Far Side* postcard like children's letters from camp, communicating nothing.

Vanishing is an act of exceptional cruelty. All she had to say was "I'm leaving, Pril." I wouldn't have tried to stop her.

Instead, my own world stopped. A decade of uncommon intimacy slammed into a concrete abutment. But this was no accident. It was a choice made by someone I believed I knew, and who knew me better than any kith or kin. Despite Scotty, despite children, I was alone, and hugely, inescapably lonely.

Ruth was my anchor. I depended on her. Cut loose I lacked ballast, drifting and foundering through days, checking my watch for passage of time, imagining what she would be doing at any given minute. Initially the time difference hampered me; then I grew accustomed to it and automatically subtracted two hours in my envisionings. Now she would be getting out of bed, wearing a T-shirt. Now she would be washing her face with Neutrogena. Now she would be drinking her coffee liberally lightened with half-and-half, and watching only the five-minute headlines brief because she hates newscaster chat. She chews an overtoasted cinnamon raisin bagel, checks *Doonesbury* in perpetual hope that the strip will tackle feminism, and, were she here, would call me about the Ann Landers letter from a woman who unknowingly married a necrophiliac. We would laugh, and compare each other's plans for the day. Now, while it was yet cool, she would weed, before she went inside to change into her riding clothes.

Our lives had been so inextricably connected that I couldn't complete or pursue the smallest task without thinking of her: selecting a video, planting impatiens in terrace pots, folding shirts, deciding what to have for dinner. I sank into an aimlessness that dogged me as I plodded through the days, walked from one room into the next, marking the steady decline of spring, the segue into summer, the fall and rise of seasons that, in other years, never failed to prompt a flurry of elation and writing.

I did not write. I, the paragon of efficiency who had organized and jealously meted out minutes, reserving errands for after school, after my "working hours," let tasks accumulate, phone calls go unanswered on the machine, found myself in grocery aisles weeknights at six o'clock, listlessly waiting for some meal to present itself to me. I began to haunt bookstores again, where idleness was accepted, expected. The focused drive to accomplish, a character trait that plagued Scotty and the children, waned, and rootlessness took its place. In a decade I had let other friendships wither, or ignored possibilities for new ones. My mother's oft-mimicked childhood adage taunted me—To have a friend you must be one—and I remembered how I had laughed when, at my guilty musing that we ought to invite a new neighbor over

165

for dinner, Ruth had joked, "Why? I've got all the friends I need."

And still no word. No letter, no call, no nothing. What I learned of Ruth I learned from Reed in short snatches he delivered with tight-lipped sarcasm from the driveway if I happened to be outside. Ruth had rented a house and found a job at the university. She wanted a divorce. No fault. He could have everything.

"Are you going to type tonight?" Bethie asked with hopeful eyes. Accustomed to falling asleep with the backdrop of clicking keys, she missed the mechanical lullaby of my typing. Instead of writing I took to playing addictive, mindless, time-consuming games of computer solitaire and Game Boy contests. Shameless diversions that came as near to blank-mindedness as any artificial means. The flashing configurations of cards or pellets or robotic men replayed themselves at night in bed on screens behind my eyelids as, exhausted by idleness but plagued with insomnia, I tried vainly to fall asleep.

I lay in bed tracing the patterns of Ruth's reasoning, the headlights of cars climbing the hill of the park spotlighting my sleeplessness. The bright beams splintered and shattered through the louvered shutters of our bedroom windows as if purposely seeking my face. Open-eyed and alert, I awaited some telepathic communication clear as the headlights to come through the darkness.

I knew why she had left. She'd been preparing for

it for years, I now saw: a life on her own, without dependence, without obligation, without husband.

But it was the answer to the other question that tormented me: Did she know when she left that she wouldn't return? I had no verbal response, no letter, but in my heart I knew the answer. She knew. That was the deepest cut. My hands twitched against the sheet with abrupt stabs of anger. Ruth had known, but she chose not to tell me, to consult or include me. *How dare you?* I wanted to shout. *How dare you?* Until sadness again overcame me. How dare I consider myself essential to her?

Because she was essential to me.

In mid-August we took our usual vacation to the beach for a week. Bedraggled and laden, we returned to Greensboro on a Sunday afternoon. As I was rinsing bicycles and rafts, Reed appeared.

"How was it?" he asked.

I turned off the spigot and straightened. "It was fine. Fun," I said warily. Our relationship had become chilly and strained. Reed didn't regard me as an adversary—he believed that I hadn't known—but in many ways I represented Ruth to him, the closest embodiment. He couldn't entirely forgive me for a crime I had no part in. "Been running?"

He nodded, dragging his sneakered toe over the concrete. I noticed the strands of gray in his bent head, more numerous since March. Reed worked nearly constantly since Ruth had left. Worked, worked out, keeping busy keeping demons at bay.

"Remember Ruth jogging that first summer we went together to the beach?" he said.

I remembered. Nearing the cottage on returning from her run, Ruth thought she saw Reed in the driveway and, grinning, lifted her shirt and raised her elastic sports bra to her neck, flashing her bare breasts at him for a come-on prank. Except that the man in the driveway was a total stranger, not Reed. We had laughed about the case of mistaken identity for years. Still looking down, Reed smiled, and I knew the pain that must have alternated with his self-doubt and anger and sorrow, swirling within in great muddy whirls. I touched his arm.

"Reed. I miss her too."

He looked up, said curtly, "Thank you so much for that small consolation."

"It wasn't intended as consolation. I'm not the enemy."

He nodded. "I know." I knew what he wanted. He wanted and needed me to explain motivation. But motivation can't be reduced to a neat package. Plucking at the ribbed neck of his T-shirt, he said, "I heard from Ruth this week."

"Is she well? The job, and apartment, and . . . everything?" Reed nodded shortly. No elaboration, no details. "Reed," I said, hesitating. "In her let-ter . . ." I laughed, an old childhood habit for disguising nervousness, for disguising the naked ache of longing. "Did Ruth . . . did she mention me?"

Even Reed sensed my abandonment, loath to deliver bad news. "No. She didn't." I turned quickly and coiled the hose. "I've signed the divorce papers, Pril. I just . . . did," he said with a kind of wonder at his own acquiescence. "But I won't let the children go and neither will Ruth." His lips set. "I'm suing for custody." I looked up swiftly to his resolute expression. "Leaving was her choice and I've accepted it and signed. But it wasn't the children's choice."

Choice. From the dangling nozzle a stream of chill water trickled into my shoe. "It's a choice," Ruth had told me, speaking of cutting the peonies. And what she was about to undertake. *Choice,* Reed was telling me now. Here is what I know of choice.

My children will eat grapes only the first two or three days after I have brought them home from the supermarket. When a dozen plucked stems begin showing, little nubs of gelatinous emptiness, when the fruit thins on the vine, or the grapes appear less plump, less perfect, the children abandon the grapes altogether, until with time the skins begin to dull and pucker and wrinkle. Then I pick the grapes myself, rinse them and place them in a different, smaller container. And with the look of perfection the children will eat the grapes once again, now that they appear separate and new, divided from the umbilicus of their stems.

As a child of four and five, Bethie played with

stuffed animals saved from my childhood, three dozen collected creatures: Steiff animals brought from F.A.O. Schwarz in New York, detailed and plush, tigers and owls and turtles combined with stiffer, beadier-eyed rabbits and kittens and pandas given as favors, won at fairs, purchased at bazaars. Always, always, Bethie chose the finer, more expensive Steiffs upon which to bestow her attention and love, her favorite names. The other animals were nameless audiences, passengers, backdrops. Is it instinct, this choice of the finer, better, more worthy of love? Or something learned, some means of selection a parent has unconsciously imparted?

Slight, distilled incidents show us the terrible arbitrariness of choice, not grandiose and philosophical quotes. And now choice had come to this. It had come down to the children. I swallowed. "Are Sloan and Grayson unhappy?"

" 'Unhappy' isn't the word. They're . . . content. With summer, this has all been like an extended vacation. But they knew nothing of Ruth's . . . intentions. Either," Reed added in a voice heavy with irony.

"Aren't you worried what a custody battle might do to them?" I asked. "All those articles about . . . children suffering through separation and . . ." I chose my words carefully, ". . . estranged parents."

But Reed seemed not to have heard me. "To walk into their rooms," he said softly, misery lending a ragged edge to his voice, "to touch their beds and toys and trophies and pictures. You can't know. I need them. They need me. I hear it in their voices over the telephone." His fists clenched. "I'm their father, goddammit!"

My perspective was different, but I knew a fraction of his anguish. My child-centered, offspring-intensive days and hours had dwindled. Solitude, which I fought for and carved out for so many years, was now mine. The greatest luxury of all, an empty house, available to me for hours at a stretch. Suddenly, impossibly, it seemed Beth and Jay were busy all day with school, friends, activities. Their eventual departure danced as a faint shadow in my peripheral vision, a first glimpse of a vague future without the demands of family. The solitude I longed for engulfed and frightened me, transforming from blessed aloneness to blank void. In small selfish moments I felt old and unproductive, with nothing to show for a life over halfway to the grave.

The children had asked, of course they had asked, why Ruth had left, why? "Sometimes," I had groped, "people, mothers, feel they have to do something different with their lives." "What different?" they demanded. "And why couldn't she do it here?" My reasons sounded ineffectual and paltry even to me. For the first time in my life I found myself wishing my children were younger, when one-sentence explanations sufficed. Beth and Jay grumbled with justifiable incomprehension, and I said, "Here's the thing for

Ruth, and for all of us. If you can't make yourself happy, no one can."

Oh, the children! I didn't blame Ruth for wanting them, and I didn't blame Reed for wanting them back. I could not hate Reed for his decision, his choice. And I could not hate Ruth for hers. "Will the children . . ." I faltered, incapable of framing a question.

"Sloan and Grayson won't be directly involved. Certainly they won't be put on the stand. Both a court-ordered therapist and the judge will talk to them outside the courtroom. Before."

"Good."

Reed stooped, picked up a Frisbee, knocked it against the car fender. Then he straightened and looked at me. "There's something else, Pril. You'll be getting a subpoena. I'm calling you as a witness. For me."

C hapter 12

F ace it, Pril," Ruth had said to me one morning. I was
still seething over an argument with Scotty the previous
evening. As with most spousal skirmishes, I now have
no idea of the issue. I remember only my frustration
and resentment with the *way* in which my husband had
hammered home his point. In all but the smallest issues
Scotty's steadfast adherence to justice and moral reasoning was so unfailingly pure, his principles so noble
and beyond reproach, that ultimately I lashed out, ar-
guing not with his point, but the manner in which it
was delivered. I heard his stolid, absolute certainty as
self-righteousness and moral piousness.

"Face it," Ruth had said. "You'll never win a fight
with Scotty. How can you? He has God on his side."

By mid-September, the hearing was scheduled for
February; Reed's "rush to the courthouse," the war

for custody, begun. The subpoena, legal notice of my unavoidable role in the Campbells's battle for their children, was delivered in early October. All that autumn, though, another war was being waged in battlefields of mute mornings, tense meals, strained silences. A war over responsibility, and blame, and the outcome of love and concern. A war that in its quiet, bloodless way was as destructive as any armed conflict. But one crucial aspect of combat was missing: I didn't know who my enemy was.

"Have you thought about what you're going to say?" Scotty asked.

"No," I said, purposely looking out the front window, away from his eyes.

"I don't believe you."

"Don't, then."

Retreating from the narrow ledge of argument, Scotty made no reply. But the vast silence of my loneliness, my refusal to discuss, was interpreted as complicity and sympathy and agreement with my closest friend's abandonment of her husband, their life. All of which it was, when I considered Ruth. When I considered Scotty, and Reed, and lawyers, and men, it was another thing altogether, and ambivalence mutated into resentment.

Oh Ruth! Had you any idea of the difficulty of my dilemma? Required to speak, and thus required to choose between duty and love, obligation and loyalty, truth and appearances? My heart lay with you, but where lay my obligation?

The topic of the impending testimony was ever-present, back-burnered but simmering with potential to boil. What I would say; how I would say it. Slight references, muttered remarks, even a newspaper article reporting a celebrity's tawdry tale of custody spawned nervous glances of apprehension between Jay and Beth. The ruses of routine, of pleasantries falsely acted, didn't fool them. I have asked the children since whether the hostility between Scotty and me, the burden of my struggle, was evident, and certainly it was, overriding the small struggles of daily living, and worse, eclipsing Jay's internalized trauma with his discovery of Roslyn's suicide seven months earlier. Adolescent behavior alone couldn't account for his worrying episodes of insolence and belligerence. And silence. In those months Jay's rebellion scabbed and festered.

"Don't fight," the children begged when stony faces and curt responses betrayed their parents' anger. "Don't. Please."

"We're not fighting," came our belated, distracted reply, no different and no more truthful than their own whined answers to our entreaties to cease their backseat bickering. Once, like a knife to the heart, Beth folded her arms and resignedly asked, "Are you two going to have another all-day fight?" The comment brought about a truce, but only temporarily.

"You've hardly said a word about this thing, Pril," Scotty commented. We were raking leaves in jagged stripes across the lawn.

"What do you want me to say?"

"Quit being evasive."

"I didn't volunteer for this job, Scotty. I didn't ask for it, you know."

Scotty straightened, palmed the rake handle. "No, and neither did Reed."

"Quit changing the subject."

"So you're just going to be a hostile witness? Is that it?"

"Hostile witness? You watch too much television." I dragged a bag of leaves to the curb, beyond earshot.

This is a fact: Most men fail to understand that in decisions and dilemmas, women want listeners, not advice. Women seek other women in discussing problems because women listen, agree or disagree, but usually, ultimately, do not attempt to pass judgment or issue rulings. It is not an equal world. Men prescribe answers and options when women really want only airtime, not advice. Sympathy, not solutions. Thus do discussions escalate into debacles, conversations into conflagrations.

After describing a day filled with minor catastrophes I once tried to explain this theory to Scotty after he had calmly listed all the things I could have, should have, done. "I stand here and tell you precisely what to do, but you never do them," he said.

I shook my head and replied, "I realize I could have done any of those things."

"Then why should I bother listening?" he said with exasperation.

"I just want you to agree."

"*Agree?*"

"I just want you to say, 'God, what a day. I'd hate to be you.'"

If just once in those months Scotty had said, "My God, what a burden. How awful for you. How do you stand it? *What* are you going to do?"

Two weeks later he tried again, lingering pointlessly as I cleared the table. Over dinner Beth had resurrected that grim game of childhood choices whispered thrillingly in the dark. "Who would you want to live with if you got to choose?" she asked Jay.

I reached for the salt, trying not to visualize the gears of Jay's brain clicking over the probable grievances he held against Scotty or me, checking to see whose list of faults was longer. While he debated, I said, "You wouldn't get to choose. There would be a judge."

"Yes, but *if*," Beth persisted.

Scotty intervened, saying severely and with finality, "Fortunately that's an issue you'll never have to worry about."

Clearly doubtful, the children swapped knowing looks across the table. They knew what fights meant. Fights meant shut faces and indistinct murmurings through bedroom walls. Fights meant divorces. Even death.

"Do you see what's going on?" Scotty asked as I wiped the counters.

"No. What?"

"Come on, Pril. That conversation at dinner, if you can call it conversation. This is affecting the children."

I pivoted. "And you think there's something I should be doing about it?"

"I think it would help if they knew where you stand."

"Stand on what?" I was being deliberately obtuse. I knew it. I was waiting for Scotty to push me. Then I could strike back and defend myself. He waited, knowing as well.

"I think it's remarkable how Ruth hasn't asked for any support," I said. "She doesn't want any of their material possessions. She hasn't required anything of Reed but her freedom."

"And the children," Scotty added dryly.

I knew what he wanted. He wanted reassurance that I would do the Right Thing. That my friendship and intimacy with Ruth would not affect my testimony at the hearing. But he wouldn't say it outright. To acknowledge my loyalty aloud would have assumed that it was even an issue, and in a completely fair world, a morally just world, Scotty's world, it would not be. I would be above that.

Something in me perversely sympathized with Scotty's plight, but I couldn't let him see my confusion, the inward turmoil between myself and my conscience. It would have given him an advantage that he would have seized. I was fighting on more than one front. I was fighting him, yes. Fighting my conscience. And in a different arena, fighting Ruth, confronting my love and loyalty to her. Scotty would have pounced, probing this chink in the armor of my silent reserve. Still, every tense exchange highlighted this irrefutable fact: You have to choose.

He looked up from the hearth, where he was laying a fire. I handed him a balled newspaper page, studied the ink smudges on my fingers. "You realize your testimony is going to weight matters heavily," he said. "You're the only witness on either side."

The box of matches felt leaden in my hand. "What makes you so sure?"

"Ruth isn't calling anyone. Reed told me."

"Why didn't he tell me?"

"For God's sakes, Pril. You were out when he called. He's not hiding anything from you. What are you doing, turning this into some male-female thing?"

"What makes him—or you—assume Ruth won't call someone?"

He stood from his crouched position and stared at me. "Have you heard from her?"

And then I had to answer. No. No word from Ruth. Nothing.

Oh Ruth! You could have done something. Stalled matters. Filed motions. Changed venue. Hired a crackerjack attorney. Fought harder, bitterer. *Something.*

I spent a day in the reference section of the main library poring over columned legalese in thick gray statute books, as if I might unearth some clue, some guidance, from the limp transparent pages. My eyes blurred from the fine print of the columned cases, the labyrinth maze of complicated footnotes and cross-references relevant to jurisdiction even more minuscule.

Hammered home repeatedly was the law: The welfare of the child is the paramount determinant of every custody decision, and a parent's love, the wishes of the child, must yield to this guiding principle. The highest authority is the best interests of the children. Moral fitness, mental and physical health, and preference of child are the three factors that affect this decision.

My hope wavered and wafted daily. It rose with each jangle of the telephone, and died with each day's mail delivery like an ember that flares and smolders and crumbles into ash. Ashes of conflict tamped and banked but still capable of igniting. Oh Ruth! You could have let me know. Called, written, in some way communicated what you were thinking, hoping, needing, wanting. So that I would know. Know how to cast my lot; in what light to cast my testimony.

Round and round and unresolved. Inwardly. Outwardly. And still Scotty never said. Never actually uttered *you should, you ought, you must*. Like a thin needle afloat on water, we maintained by surface tension alone. Until December, with its minefield of hazardous, high-strung holidays.

Equal and fair, Scotty and I annually rotated where we spent Christmas. That year it was Scotty's family we visited, and coincidentally, his four older sisters were coming too. The house was noisily chaotic with adults and offspring, gear and gifts and food.

Christmas Eve afternoon I returned from a walk and discovered a note on the refrigerator that everyone had trooped to the mall for last-minute shopping. It was a ritual outing that fueled Scotty's Christmas spirit. The hectic crowds of package-toting, pink-cheeked shoppers aroused no frantic worry about finding presents, but infused him with gaiety instead. I plugged in the tree lights to dispel the gathering dusk and regarded the bulky mounds of presents. Of course the crowds didn't worry Scotty, I thought with irritation. Why should they? I'd already done all the searching and shipping and wrapping and packing, freeing him from responsibility.

In the kitchen the dishwasher thumped and churned with the effort of the second of its three daily cycles. A Whitman's Sampler of candy lay open on the counter, its snug virgin configuration of chocolates ransacked for dependable caramel squares. Empty dark-brown fluted holders were scattered among suspect pieces whose undersides were fingernail punctured or peeled to reveal their jelly or nougat interiors. Not even particularly hungry, I located a reliable nut chew. Beaded with condensed fat, the country ham we'd eaten for lunch was still uncovered on its platter, and before going to our room I clumsily carved away a thick stringy slice, burgundy red and so salty it stung my lips.

With everyone home, Scotty and I were staying in his old childhood bedroom over the garage, an afterthought renovation when Scotty was eventually routed from the main house upstairs as his sisters required and claimed all available space.

Filled with desk, bookshelf, beds, and bureau, the room was small and blockily angular to accommodate the original lines of the house and an added bath. The ceiling was only a two-foot flat strip between sloping walls of the roofline. A dowel under the eaves served as closet, high enough for shirts and blazers but not for my dresses, so they hung forlornly from a hook over the bathroom door along with Scotty's first skinny, never-discarded rep ties.

Any pictures were necessarily hung at neck level, though there were few enough of those: two or three framed athletic and academic awards, a black-and-white photograph of Scotty with a friend at Pat O'Brien's bar in New Orleans some Mardi Gras before I was, literally, in the picture. Below it the scarred wooden desk bore a melamine ashtray filled with pennies and the requisite green blotter gouged with shredded black sinkholes from doodling fountain pens. Old yearbooks were stacked in a corner, within whose fake leather-grained covers were rows of pictures and scribbled messages I had pored over when I first stayed in

182

Scotty's room, finally granted admittance to his personal domain through the sanction of marriage. Greedily, lovingly, I had examined and touched every inanimate object as though it were a totem, imbued with some magic, some key to better knowing and thus more fully possessing Scotty.

As a newlywed I found the room cozy, a refuge and retreat secluded from the mania of family. It charmed me, as did everything about my husband: his hands, his habits, his possessions. His goodness. Now the room seemed claustrophobic and confining, stale-smelling and underheated, cluttered with furniture and belongings. Scotty had unpacked, as usual, no matter the length of stay. As though he'd never moved out, as though they weren't temporary quarters, his folded underwear—folded by me—lay in the upper bureau drawer beside two neatly rolled belts, coiled like cobras. I never unpack. Clunky unfoldable items—hair dryer, jewelry case, shoes—spilled from my open suitcase.

I stood at the foot of one of the twin beds and thought of the summons and Ruth, of our old eye-rolling disdain for men's refusal to share beds. The bleak wintry landscape, the stalky black tree trunks beyond the window intensified my melancholy. A neighboring family was apparently leaving town, or had left—perhaps to go skiing, like Ruth's ruse—evidenced by the sad sight of their Christmas tree already discarded at the curb, an upended bristly cone. I thought too of Roslyn, the tragedy of her death, her final futile efforts at holiday cheer. Acts of desperation, like abortion, suicide, and flight. The raw gray afternoon seeped through the windowpanes, chilling my fingers, and I turned away, deciding to take a hot shower.

Scotty's powder, razor, and deodorant stick were lined predictably on the bathroom shelf beside old shampoo bottles whose plastic shoulders were cloudy with age and disuse. White dust of carelessly over-applied powder coated the sink and sill and tiles. Like Berk's once no doubt did for Roslyn, like Reed's did for Ruth, my husband's pale sifted presence remained in every niche or crevice, enraging me in ways I couldn't explain.

Too far from the utility room, the shower never received an adequate supply of pressure or hot water. Too late, I remembered the dishwasher's greedy claim of water, and midshower I was forced to shave my legs in tepid, then cold water, which raised goose pimples I sliced off unawares. Bloody and burned, my legs itched and stung; my mouth and throat were parched from salty ham and sugar.

The cold, the pain, the room, the joyless day, the coming twenty-four-hour conveyor of gaiety I was expected to join; suddenly it was all too much to endure. The ash flamed. Cursing, I brusquely emptied my duffel to find my robe, then sat on the bed and slathered lotion on the chapped skin of my legs, where rough hairs still sprouted. Below, footsteps mounted the stairs: Scotty, exuding outdoor cold and cheer, his jacket lapel pinned with a goggling, bug-eyed Santa Claus. He looked at my nicked and trickling legs.

"What did you do to yourself?"

"It's not what I did. It's the shower, there's never any hot water, it's too busy competing with all your sisters' bathrooms, not to mention the dishwasher. And thanks for lifting the toilet seat. I fell in. What happens—you come home and revert to unmarried status?"

Scotty looked at me with mild amusement. "Get a grip, Pril."

Goaded by his impassivity, I slung the towel over the headboard. "You know what? I hate your mother's house. I hate this room, the way we get stuck up here. And I hate having to do that Pollyanna present-picking thing with all your sisters."

Scotty stood there, dumbfounded by my outburst. "Look at that." I swept my arms about, indicating the walls, even the narrow ceiling wallpapered with a somber blue-and-gold print depicting soldiers and military equipment of historic wars—uniformed soldiers, cannons, rifles, pistols. "This cheesy wallpaper. So typical, so macho. Guns and combat, some little boy fantasy theme. Wouldn't Ruth love that? Wouldn't Ruth have a few thousand well-chosen words to say on the subject of your boyhood wallpaper?"

Scotty's eyes narrowed. "That's what this is about, then. Ruth." I clamped my lips together. He sat beside me on the bed. "What are you going to say, Pril?" he asked slowly, deliberately.

"I'll answer the questions," I answered mulishly, and resorted to childish retort. "What's it to you, anyway?"

"Are you going to tell the truth?"

"What are you implying? That I would lie? Thank you so very much for your high opinion."

"You realize that you have a huge responsibility to—"

"Oh, please," I interrupted him, disgusted. "Cut the subtlety and say it, Scotty. You've been dying to for months now. Let's get it all out on the table. You want me to throw all the weight of my testimony on Reed's behalf."

His fingers tensed against his knees. "You *are* Reed's witness."

"Maybe I'm just his witness because he tagged me first, before Ruth could!"

"But she didn't, did she?" I turned away. Scotty gentled his voice. "Put yourself in Reed's place. Wouldn't you fight it?"

"I'm not questioning his reason to fight it. I hate that term."

Scotty ignored the aside. "Suppose it was me who was out on the lam with Beth and Jay. You're damn straight you would fight."

I gaped. "Out on the lam? *Out on the lam?*"

He rose and strode to the window. "Are you going to argue that what Ruth did was acceptable? Ruth is basically a renegade housewife. You think it's okay. Don't you? You think it's acceptable!"

"*A renegade housewife?*" I hissed. "Try straight-jacketed. You don't know anything."

"Oh, I see, but *you* do. Pril, the all-knowing." He chopped the air with his hand. "I know what I see. I know what happened. I know that Ruth Campbell picked up and packed up and left without so much as a good-bye and waltzed off into the sunset to find herself. Didn't that kind of thing go out with the sixties?"

"And didn't that kind of chauvinistic asshole attitude go out with the sixties?" I jerked the knots from my wet hair. "Why doesn't Reed just leave her alone? Ruth has made a new life for herself without obligating him, or submitting to him or emasculating him."

Scotty's face twisted with disgust. "This is Ruth, not an ideology! Leave the feminist bullshit out of this!"

"What's the matter, feeling threatened?"

"Explain to me how this is different from Berk, Pril. Greener grass, abandonment. Tell me." He nodded his head slowly, the wise sage manner infuriating me.

"Jesus, Scotty. Berk was having an affair. He lied, he cheated, he didn't love her, he used and manipulated Roslyn."

"Pril. I know how you feel about Ruth."

"No, you don't! You have no idea. It's not within your capacity of emotions."

His expression grew wide-eyed. "Sometimes I don't think I know you."

Susan S. Kelly

"Maybe you don't," I snapped. He turned his back to me, fiddled with the mug of pencils on his desk. "I'm trying to consider Ruth," I said evenly. "What's best for her. What she's thinking."

"Ruth never cared an iota what anyone thinks. That's her problem."

"Shut up, Scotty. It's not a problem! It's not conforming. It's not accepting things as they are. Thank God for people like Ruth."

"So you think what she did was right? Permissible, then, even admirable. Just how far does your holy loyalty extend? Do you miss Ruth so much, do you love her so much, that you'll perjure yourself?"

"It's what Ruth *needed*. Is that so despicable? Or haven't you ever needed anything," I said bitterly.

"This isn't only about what *Ruth* needs. This involves other people."

His tone was so smugly reasonable I wanted to smack him. "Don't try to shame me by trying to appear noble and selfless," I said with withering scorn. "And kindly spare me your holier-than-thou indignation. My God, she's already lain down and let Reed have it all. Isn't that a kind of selflessness as well?"

It was Scotty's turn to sneer. "Define 'all.'"

Stone-faced, I pulled on socks.

"This isn't about taking sides, Pril." His tone was gravelly with sternness.

My own voice was ragged and shrill. "Quit using my goddamn name!" I plugged in the hair dryer and clicked it on, purposely drowning him out. "Don't

188

condescend to me like I'm some simpleton too stupid
to comprehend your irrefutable logic. Of *course* it's
about taking sides! Someone is going to win! What
do you think it's about?"

"It's about what is right!"

"And you of course are the eternal expert on that!"

"Look at me, Pril."

"That's right. Patronize me like I'm one of the children. *Look at me, Pril,*" I mimicked with mincing
sarcasm, and, snapping off the dryer, pitched it into
the suitcase.

Scotty took a deep breath and glared at me. "You
know what I think? I think you feel guilty because
you know what you should say. Admit it, Pril." He
grabbed my wrist. "Isn't good old guilt making you
talk this way?"

And then I hit him, wrenching from his grasp and
lunging with every fiber of my strength contained in
balled and knotted fists. I struck him with six months
of withheld grief and confusion and frustration. His
body was meaty, rubbery beneath my furious blow.

Scotty stood still, his arms dangling at his sides,
and looked at the floor. "Would it help to kick me in
the balls?" he asked softly.

I backed away, shamed, and collapsed on the too-
soft mattress, clapping my hands to my eyes. Anger
dissolved into tears of regret, exhaustion, and always,
the dilemma of my decision; still, after that terrible
scene, no closer to closure. "It felt like socking a
steak," I said miserably. "I'm sorry for that . . . low

blow." Scotty swept the towel, the jeans, the sweater from the bed and, sitting beside me, pulled my hands away from my face and held them between his own.

"My blows were just as low. I'm sorry," he said. "I push too hard." He gazed out the window. "I suppose it seems a simple choice to me. But choice is never simple."

"It's so goddamn complicated," I said, choking, "choice." The choice of grapes and chocolates and stuffed animals, the choice of leaving, of death by one's own hand, the choice of judge, the choice between duty and friend, of what we choose to tell and how we choose to tell it.

Scotty rubbed my fingers. The diamonds of my wedding band winked in the weak overhead light. "This is about independence," I said. "Not from Reed in particular. From everything." My voice weakened, cracked. "Oh, Scotty. She left me, too." I sat on the bed in my husband's childhood room and wept. Wept for our fighting, the hurtful accusations and denouncements, the unforgivable things husbands and wives and friends say and do to each other, the equally unforgivable, unattainable things they expect from one another. And for Ruth and Reed, the children, and for my plight.

"I know," Scotty said. "I know." He held me close, until my tears were spent.

"You smell like your mother's car," I grumbled finally, snuffling tiredly into the collar of his shirt.

Against my cheek, I felt his face stretch into a

smile. "Shall I tell her that, along with the wallpaper, and the hot water, and the Pollyanna picking?"

Below I heard the stirring of family: voices, clinking dishes, carols from the stereo. Christmas. "Remember how you used to dip your boot soles in flour and walk them across the living room floor from the fireplace," I asked, "as if Santa had walked through the house with snow on his feet?" Scotty nodded, his chin bumping my scalp. "Roslyn told me once that what she really wanted on Christmas Day was for her children to come down the stairs and fall over in a dead faint when they saw everything they got."

Scotty pulled me onto his lap, my pathetic bloody legs and damp robe. I let him. "What else?" he asked. An electronic beep chirped from the thyroid-eyed Santa pinned to his coat.

"I remember when I thought you were everything." He laid his finger across the flashing red eyes, blinding Santa, and held me tighter. "And we none of us are, or should have to be. You to me, the children to us. Ruth to me," I whispered.

"And what else," Scotty coaxed, unjudgmental and unfazed by my non-sequitur dialogue, accepting its origins.

"I pick friends who are not caretakers."

"Because you take care of yourself," he said. I squeezed my eyes tightly shut, and he added. "Or try to."

I sighed hugely and hiccuped. "You're going to hate what I'm giving you for Christmas."

He tapped my thigh. "You got marketed again, didn't you?" It was an old joke, originating with a hideous sweater I'd mail-ordered for him one year because the model had looked so good in it. "Those catalog pictures suckered you in again, didn't they? They sucked Ruth in."

No anger flared in me. Only immense sadness, and longing. "No they didn't, Scotty. They had nothing to do with Ruth going. She knows herself better than you do, or I." I thought of Ruth's gifts to me last Christmas. She'd given me a book of postcards featuring May Sarton quotes and photographs, and Carolyn Heilbrun's *Writing a Woman's Life,* which I had yet to read. I'd given her a coffee mug depicting a cartoon drawing of shepherds, wise men, and animals clustered around the manger. "It's a girl!" one of them was shouting.

Scotty nuzzled my neck, reading my mind in the room's quiet gloom. "Do you remember what I gave Ruth for Christmas two years ago?"

I looked at him expectantly, shook my head no.

"The boxing nun." He smiled. That was right. A hand puppet dressed in black habit and wimple with grinning wizened face. Under the dress was a finger lever that, when pulled, raised a boxing-gloved hand with a rabbit punch. "Picked it out all by myself."

I laughed aloud. She'd taken the duking nun to every occasion. Did Ruth have it still? Did she use the coffee mug? "I had forgotten you were funny," I said.

He gingerly laid his palm on my calf. "And occasionally even handy. Would you like a styptic pencil?"

"And some water. I'm so thirsty. From the chocolate and the ham. And the crying."

"Stay," he said. "I'll be back."

*C*hapter 13

It was so utterly, utterly civil.

"All you need to know," Mr. Barber, Reed's skinny, kindly, clueless attorney said to me, "is that people don't go to court to necessarily tell the truth about everything. The 'truth' in a courtroom is just a construction of effects. There is no such thing as simple truth as long as its presentation can be shaped, or perverted, or invented. Justice is impersonal."

I know, I wanted to tell him. I have raised children. Children who by nature adhere to the literal, actual letter of the law, not its spirit or intent. I know about versions of the truth, how blame is placed and perceived.

The courtroom was a windowless cube whose combination of linoleum floors and cherry paneling was warmly, strangely sterile. The ceiling's chalk-colored acoustical tiles were splotched with irregular holes of gray in the spongy surface, as though mice or moths had gnawed them.

No doubt Ruth was unsurprised that there were only three females in the room: Ruth, her lawyer, and myself. I was observant of that also, the result of so many years with Ruth. The cacophony of my thoughts and hammering heart drowned out the preliminary legalese as I sat across the chasm of courtroom aisle watching Ruth, transfixed by her pretty profile, the back of her head, as she bent toward her attorney.

So near, so distant. And what had I expected: that we would share a sitter for the hearing? Meet for coffee beforehand? Ask her what she was wearing? Still surprising me, Ruth wore a sweater set of all things, synonymous with the submissive fifties. Perhaps I anticipated the suede, fringed Robert Redford Sundance coat, or a slick nylon skiing jacket. I wore houndstooth, a suit I'd bought at Ruth's urging in Loehmann's.

"I don't know, Ruth," I'd said, buttoning up the jacket, stroking the velvet lapels. I hated undressing in that fluorescent public corral, encircled by walls of accusing, unflattering mirrors like consciences, which highlighted every imperfection.

"What?"

"Wearing a suit seems so . . ." —I hesitated— "grown-up."

Ruth laughed. "Pril," she'd said. "You *are* grown-up."

How do they do it, murderers and rapists and robbers? How do they face their victims, the families of their victims, the same features they have bludgeoned or brutalized etched in bereaved visages ten feet from their chair? I sat there, an enthroned and summoned captive, and sought her eyes. Searching for grief, sorrow, anger, regret, I found none. I like to think I saw love there, communicated through her radiant calm composure.

Outwardly reserved, I was inwardly alert and adversarial, taut and tensed, and Ed Barber, for all his avuncular obsequiousness, intuited it. "Don't volunteer any unnecessary information," he had advised. "Simply answer the questions." And so I did. Yes, Reed was involved in his children's lives, in PTA and scouts, coached their teams. Yes, yes, I responded, affirming the attorney's exploration of Reed's stellar paternal qualities.

And then he changed the subject, to Ruth.

Nearly every question asked of me has been, as the judge was fond of saying, otherwise noted in earlier pages. All but the final one.

"Mrs. Henderson, do you know of any viable, believable reason Mrs. Campbell might leave her husband and take her children from him?"

"No."

"And so, Mrs. Henderson, you had no idea, you never knew, of Ruth Campbell's intention to take her children. To leave Greensboro permanently?"

"I can't see what difference that makes."

"Just answer the question if you please, Mrs. Henderson."

"No."

He looked down, shuffled papers on the gleaming table.

"Can I go now?"

"One last question." He smiled falsely, indulging my impatience, my reluctance. "You have children, do you not, Mrs. Henderson?"

"Two."

He nodded sagely. "In your opinion, Mrs. Henderson, was Mrs. Campbell a good mother?"

I started with an involuntary shudder, a tremble of fear. A good mother. My eyes flew to Ruth, and met only her downcast head, her lowered lashes. A Good Mother.

"Pardon?" I stammered, buying seconds. Then Ruth looked up, slowly knit her fingers on the table, and, nodding slightly, smiled at me.

"Mrs. Henderson?" he prompted. "Did you hear the question? Was Ruth Campbell a good mother to her children?"

Ask the children, I nearly replied, blithely secure. But swiftly as that thought surfaced it was replaced with terror. Wait, no, please. Don't ask them. What will they remember, the children, those judges conferred by genes? When one is innocent of the heinous sins decreed and agreed upon by law and society—

adultery, drugs, drink, abuse, neglect—what standards remain for reckoning? Will there be blame, or gratitude? What do children remember?

Will Beth remember that I didn't buy sufficient PTA magazine subscriptions or Fun Day raffle tickets to qualify her for a tape recorder, or will she remember the times I gave her money for the tinkling ice-cream truck at dusk? Will Jay remember that I didn't drive every field trip at school or come to his class and help him make a totem pole out of recycled products? Or will he remember the nights I took him to the library for the last-minute report on Antarctica, the nights at the mall searching for Styrofoam spheres to construct a solar system dangling from a wire hanger? With what litany of grievances and omissions will they condemn me?

Or will they thank us? Will Sloan remember Ruth plunging her hands into the still-black ooze of the chartered bus's closeted commode, choking with fumes of exhaust and disinfectant, to fish out her daughter's dropped glasses on a Girl Scout trip? Will Grayson recall that his mother always had flowers on the kitchen table and served a meat and two vegetables nearly every night for dinner, or will he recall that she forbade him to take canned sodas to school with his bag lunch?

Will my children remember there were days I didn't touch them all day long? They won't remember, because they will never know, that on those nights I watched the porcelain perfection of their faces and limbs in slumbered repose and wept at their bedside, stricken by my inadvertent neglect of maternal touch. For what will they hold us responsible, condense and resurrect later as evidence to accuse, to define, to thank God for, to pinpoint as then, *then* was I blessed, encouraged, ruined?

"Mrs. Henderson?" Ed Barber repeated gently.

I remember. I remember Ruth and me patiently teaching the girls to tie their shoes, something about a rabbit going down a hole over and over and over. And I remember a toddling Jay whining throughout an entire day, suffering my scoldings yet unable to tell me of his pain, that his baby toe was folded backward in his tennis shoe because I had hurriedly crammed his foot in.

One hears that personalities are shaped, created, imprinted before we are three, a theory both terrifying and reassuring. I'd like to ask, "Is it true? Do you remember?" but am afraid to. Glimpses of what they remember come through now occasionally, the obliging child who will reveal, "I remember that time you made me invite someone over to play I didn't like." And thankfully with age they understand blame as well. "I remember the time I drew on the walls and blamed it on Bethie because she couldn't talk," Jay has laughingly confessed.

I remember making chocolate pudding and allowing the children to slosh milk into it and spoon and stir it like mud; how Ruth demonstrated sucking Jell-O down her throat without chewing to the screamed laughter of all the children, and me. I remember Sloan and Grayson's plastic placemats of the United States, the states in bright primary colors with starred capital cities and Ruth's premeal commandment: "Put your milk on Maine!"

Ask them, I wanted to say. Ask the children how they learned and who played Thumbkin and Crazy 8s and Chutes and Ladders with them. Ask them if they can sing "When Irish Eyes Are Smiling," "You Are My Sunshine," "This Land Is Made for You and Me." "The Ship *Titanic*." *The rain came down and nearly drove those—clap!—animals crazy, crazy, children of the Lord.*

Don't ask. Don't ask about the day I drove carpool, the shrieks and bragging and bathroom talk finally beyond my endurance, when Jay turned around and said, "Be quiet! My mother doesn't like children." Don't ask about Ruth, on a rampage, saying grimly to me, "I don't consider it a day unless I've made someone cry."

I kept my children safe, didn't I? Didn't I keep them from darting into the street by pointing out a dead squirrel, flattened and bloody, veiny strings of bluish guts trailing from its matted fur, and say, "See? That's what happens when you go into the street." Don't ask.

Will they know as mothers we tried? Tried to be equal in dividing chores, to be fair in assigning allowances. Will you remember having to take out the garbage, or will you remember that I took you to the dump one steamy summer afternoon because you wanted to know where the garbage went?

What skewering, maiming remark will they remember? Will it be Ruth's exasperated aside to Grayson the afternoon he complained that everything had gone wrong: "Well, Grayson, I guess I'd just go fall on a knife." Or will it be mine at five o'clock after an endless day of winter confinement when still another request was made, for an umbrella, a game, cookies, crayons. "Leave me alone, can't you? Pretend like I'm dead."

Even the Perfect Mothers suffer from heartbreaking childhood candor. Even the supermoms. Even the Roslyns. "I have a theory," David had told her one night in bed, after a long tearful struggle with the rigors of fourth-grade homework. "I have a theory that when there are three children in a family, one is always dumb," he said with soft innocent certainty, felling his mother, crumpling her with remorse. "Sometimes I don't think you like me," Bethie once said wistfully to me.

"Watch it," Reed once said. "Pril remembers everything."

My mother has told me that when I entered kindergarten the teachers complained that there was nothing they could teach me because I already knew all the finger plays and nursery rhymes and chanted ditties. But I do not remember these accomplishments, testimonials of my mother's attention. What I remember is her clearly derogatory comment one afternoon that I smelled like school. What I hold her liable for is forgetting to pick me up from the movies one Saturday so that I sat through *Ben Hur* twice. I remember her obsessively reading the Pulitzers one year to the exclusion of everything else, and not giving me money to go to Florida with my friends for spring break.

Ruth remembered her mother giving her a home perm to entertain her while she was home for two weeks waiting for chicken pox scabs to fall off. " 'Failed' is too kind a description," Ruth sighed. "My hair was singed, and stank, not to mention an altogether different color. There I sat on my mother's high four-poster bed, a poster child for kinks and calamine."

Do I wish such a photographic and judging mind on my own offspring, capable of condemning or redeeming me? Do we all of us have such stories, or are just writers cursed and blessed with ineradicable memory?

"This is what my mother told me once," I said to Ruth. " 'You were my smartest child, Pril. You had the highest IQ, the greatest academic capacity. Holly'—my younger sister—'wasn't as intelligent as you, but she was the one with superb leadership traits. And Frances'—the youngest—'had *both* smarts and leadership, but never fully realized either one.' " I licked my lips. "Damning with faint praise is what my mother considers a compliment. To her, and to me."

"When I came home from college one vacation my mother found a pack of cigarettes in my blazer pocket," Ruth said. "You know what she said to me? 'Oh, Ruth,' she said. 'I'm so glad you're smoking. It's so becoming.' "

I had laughed and said, "Is that the best you can do?"

"Actually, no," Ruth answered, her voice echoing as she leaned into the washing machine's cavernous maw. "One time, on the way home from taking my brothers, James and Chas, to summer camp, my parents thought I was asleep, lying across the backseat. But I'd stayed awake on purpose to watch the sway-back telephone lines outside the window rise and dip, like an unwinding ball of string. And I liked to smell my father's cigarette when he lit it with the car lighter. That good leaf-burning autumn scent." She paused and draped six black socks over an accordioned rack. She was still air-drying Reed's socks then, the way he liked them. "Up in the front seat my parents began discussing divorce." Ruth looked at me. "The possibilities. The logistics.

"My mother said, 'But what about the children?' and my father took a deep drag and replied, 'You can have James and I'll take Chas, and Ruth . . . well, let's flip for Ruth.' "

I was mute with the brutality of the cruel, bald remark, for Ruth's suffering. "I've never told anybody

that. Not even my women's group," she said, smiling
wanly at me. "For the sake of the children," she repeated, sighing, whatever pain the memory evoked
stashed and stunted within her. "The next year *I* went
to camp. And the next seven years too." She walked
to the kitchen window, pressed her palms flat against
the panes, and looked over the backyard where
Bethie and Sloan were playing a favorite make-believe
game: Lost Children. "Good old Kiahwassee."

Ruth opened the window and raised her voice,
singsonging a nonsense chant I'd neither heard nor
thought of in twenty years; an Indian call wailed at
odd times throughout the rocky hills of Kiahwassee,
from the cabins of Tower Up six-year-olds clear out
to Paradise. Age had no claim to this mournful mys-
tic communication; it was available to any camper
with the perseverance to memorize the syllables and
the guts to shout it out, not knowing whose high girl-
ish voice would answer. "Hie low eeny meeny cow
cow mmm chow chow kee wah wah!" Ruth sang out.

And from the yard, from Sloan, came the unmistakable response. "Shim sham hilly billy wam tam
tommy oh!" Ruth had taught her daughter, painstakingly rehearsing and repeating for days until she knew
it. Ruth turned from the window, shot me a grin and
a thumbs-up. "Still works."

The lawyer didn't phrase the question the way I
wanted. *Ask me*, I thought. *Ask me whether her children can call each other with our camp signal. Ask me
if they know hie low.* Before and below me Ruth nod-

ded again and smiled, that fearless, thousand-volt grin I'd witnessed a thousand times; a smile that encompassed every spare and silly and significant moment of our friendship. My father was fond of quotes and maxims, his own and others. "You don't own children," he used to say. "You just look after them for a while."

"*Is,*" I said, "*is.*"

"*What?*"

And then I spoke too loudly, too swiftly, suggesting hurry to cover a lie, an inability to decide. I used the wrong tense, implying a phase of history, not the present. I protested too much. But it was none of these. It was because I was so very very sure.

"*Yes,*" I blurted. "*Ruth was a wonderful mother.*"

And after the dread and apprehension, the searching and the waiting, my entire testimony took ten minutes.

The judge's decision took fifteen. Sloan and Grayson Campbell were to live with their father. To his credit Reed didn't clap, grin, or gesture. And to hers, Ruth did not cry.

*C*hapter 14

WOWOWOWOWOWO the siren screams two streets over, the noise of fear and panic. I flinch. Little things make me jumpy now, still. I mistake the scamper of squirrels over the roof for an intruder in the attic, the staccato ring of a woodpecker's beak against our impenetrable gutters for a crowbar at a window. A lone stroller or bicycler suddenly looming behind me on the sidewalk startles me. With the children in school all day, with Ruth and Roslyn gone, I lock the door even when I'm inside the house.

The neighborhood has changed. Trains still slice along the track, and the garbage truck still grumbles and wheezes past, but there are no children left to gather, to clamber through the kudzu, scramble out the door and to the curb for watching. Once, the children would have been fascinated by the revolving concrete churner at work in the neighboring driveway, the implied concept of perpetual motion contained in its cylindrical twirl, but they are no longer children. "You have to keep moving or you stiffen up and die," Ruth said once, "like sharks and concrete mixers." I thought she was talking about marriage, not herself.

Neither are there children left to play Beauty Parlor, not that I could participate. A month ago I ruthlessly had my hair chopped to copy a picture I'd covertly ripped out and stolen from a library magazine. "Seriously spur!" Ruth would chortle appreciatively. "But I look like Jane Eyre!" I'd moan.

"Mom!" Jay calls from his bedroom. His voice is weary, tinged with boredom and exasperation. I know that tone. I've heard it in answer to my commands to the children to straighten their rooms, heard it from Scotty during arguments, heard it from the prosecutor at the hearing.

I go to find him, relieved at least that he's doing homework. With a nearly proud display of mediocrity, Jay had announced, "Straight hooks!" before showing us the line of Cs on his last report card. "Need help with something?" I ask. But it isn't homework. Over his slouched shoulders I see the printed form the psychologist has asked him to complete.

The spaces for responses are largely blank, though here and there Jay's messy handwriting has exceeded the margins. "This!" he says, and points to a question. DO YOU WORRY ABOUT MASTURBATION? it reads. I stifle the impulse to laugh. "Mom, what's oral sex?"

Grayson had asked Ruth at nine. "It's a myth," she'd blithely returned.

I glance at the preceding question. WHAT DO YOU BELIEVE YOUR MOTHER EXPECTS OF YOU? *That I do the best I can,* Jay's scrawl reads. Beneath the next question—WHAT DO YOU BELIEVE YOUR FATHER EXPECTS OF YOU?—he has written: *To bust my ass.*

Hoping for a shocked response, he grins wickedly up at me, a sarcastic slant to his eyes. "Just put 'No,' Jay," I tell him gently, refusing to be provoked. He resents the appointments, and though Scotty questions the expense of professional help, he agreed at my insistence. Jay has told me of frightening dreams in which his fingers have grown thick and webbed and laced, like baseball gloves.

"You were right to call," Dr. Martin agreed when I called eight months ago, telling him of Jay's increasingly poor grades and troubling hostility; when I explained the dual traumas of Ruth's leaving and Roslyn's death. "People count too long and too strong on the oblivion of children," he had said. I want to seek out and extinguish Jay's smoldering tendencies now, before they ignite. Before my son becomes irretrievable. We'll take no more chances on situations' correcting themselves.

I went to the video store last night, rewarding myself for a day of good writing. I still haven't watched the movie, and it will be after midnight before I return it. Scotty will be asleep, but I don't mind the late hour. "Why don't you just wait until tomorrow and pay the overdue fee?" Scotty asks. A thin current of sadness flows between us, but there is a peculiar strength to our marriage, an unspoken realization and agreement concerning the fragility of happiness, the flow and corrosion of everyday rituals. "We complement each other," he has said on occasion. "With an 'e' not an 'i.' "It's principle," I have said on another. "With an 'i' not an 'a.' "

But still bound by deadlines, the rules of others and my own, I'll venture out to MovieMax at midnight anyway. Too, I like scanning the shelves of films, rediscovering titles significant to me during some earlier, different phase of my life. I like watching, observing, standing shoulder to shoulder and listening to the knots of people: paunched older couples debating the merits of dated musicals and comedies, slouched and weaving teenagers who prowl the new releases, loners like myself who search the drama section. The gays are easy to spot, particularly the lesbians, and I think of that old groundless rumor about Ruth. Even with that blessedly brief and ultimately comical episode she taught me something. "I had no idea there was such a fine line between the definitions of 'friendship' and 'relationship,' " she'd commented, "did you?"

Ever the observer, I watch the video browsers, and long to ask them all what they are looking for. The humanity of these strangers comforts me, the proof that life pulses on, constant and continuing beyond the stilled homes and cricket-filled yards of my neighborhood. The movies, the people, all remind me of Ruth. So much does. Still. Still and despite the continuing absence of letter, of call, of explanation. It has been a year since we saw one another in court. Two years since she left me. I still wait for the mailman.

I write all the time now, steadily and contentedly, without compulsion or dread. A book is finished, agented and accepted. Thus I am affirmed. But I still haven't written what I set out to write initially, because I can't define my subject.

I do not want to write about what people do and why. I want to write about the way candlelight casts a net of ethereal gold upon the hair and lives and history of women at a dinner party table. The look of the light on the jewelry, the collars, the stockinged legs, its forgiving golden hue so like the dimmed overhead light of chartered buses ferrying us back to camp from a dance with a neighboring boys' camp, glowing over giggled confidences and sly looks and budding crushes. They are the same girls at the table, though they are not the same girls. What are the differences in their dreams and drives and hopes and expectations, and what has been forfeited or forgotten or waylaid that they imagined they wanted so badly? That delicate and muted and golden light—not a shiny glare of daylight; not a chemical fluorescence that frosts and cheapens. I want to capture the way it looks, and what is lost. Accidental, unintentional, everyday tragedies.

"But you can write about that. You can do both," Ruth said. And so I have.

Sometimes I become so absorbed with writing that I forget what I'm doing. I find my hairbrush in the freezer, earrings in a bowl of fruit. It is like those old days of missing her, when I would glance at the clock and find four hours had elapsed.

I still work in a corner of my bedroom cluttered with papers and books, stacks of typewritten sheets and sticky notelets of scribbled dialogue, images, titles, even names for possible fictional characters. *"Real writing"* reads one, a childhood term for cursive. *"Kimono arms. Moles across street"* reads another message, a cryptic arcane cipher to anyone but myself. And perhaps Ruth. I debated renting an office in one of the nondescript cookie-cutter buildings downtown, a "hundred-dollar hideout," Scotty said. But I never did.

"You could never live alone, Pril," Ruth once said. "You need people too much." The comment, the electric quality of her candor, had both annoyed and gladdened me, that Ruth knew me so thoroughly. But of course she was right about that too. She realized my dependency on her long before I did. "You have to be ruthless," she said. That is what I became, what she herself determined. Ruth-less.

As I write, her asides and advice—wry or earnest, taunted or tender—revisit and haunt me. "I read somewhere," she said, "that every author is permitted to write one novel in first person."

"Why?"

"Because third person is easier to read, easier to escape into. First person is constrictive. Only allows you to fully get in the brain of one character. And because first person novels—and first novels—are usually highly autobiographical." She had cut her eyes at me.

The smells leap out at me unexpectedly, from unlikely sources. Ruth is there in the rich animal scent of leather as I fumble through my handbag for keys. She was there in the earthy, dusty smell of Jay's hair as I leaned over him. She is there in my watchband, scented with hundreds of mornings of dabbed perfume. The slight aromas stun me with the ferocity of longing they inspire, the sharp smack of instant awareness like the child guards, still attached to drawers and cabinets throughout the house, which break my nails when I come hurriedly across them. Does she think of me when she smells old book bindings?

Years ago, Scotty accused me of being a scorekeeper, of keeping track of who spent more time with the children—doing homework, looking after them while running weekend errands, who had been absent the most weeknights. Mean, incessant tallying of hours and time. Perhaps I was, and am. But if I am, I know that in the final tallying, not time but forgiveness is what matters. Forgiving parents, children, friends for—in that lovely archaic language of the old prayer book—what they have done, for what they have left undone. Our manifold sins and wickedness. I forgave Ruth for not telling me. For leaving me. Her deliberate independence allowed me mine. She knew that. I didn't. Perhaps Ruth has forgiven me as well.

I didn't see him approach. I'd turned to wipe the dust from a framed picture, my sleeve leaving a clear trail on the glass. The mail drops through the slot, scatters on the floor, and I stoop to retrieve it. Bills, a flyer, the inevitable catalogs with their cunning, captivating scenarios. And floating between them, caught between their glossy covers, a letter postmarked Idaho.

Inside, folded twice, is a thin slip of paper, a black-and-white page torn from a magazine. It's a picture of Audrey Hepburn: young, exquisitely lovely, with close-cropped hair, the famous wide smile and luminous dark eyes. She is wearing tight black capri pants, ballet slippers, and a simple white shirt, and the photographer has caught her graceful body and delighted expression in midstep, midhop, a furled umbrella as her only dance partner.

In the corner of the page is Ruth's slanted scribble. There's no "Dear Pril," no greeting; she hasn't written my name. *"We somehow missed being 'gamine'!"* she has written. I envision her grin, the wistful ruefulness. *"Remember Audrey crying in the taxi? Knowing she has to go? Remember the leaving? The princess has to choose which life she'll live. We left the most important one out of our movie list—* Roman Holiday!*"*

213

"What's for dinner, Mom?" Jay calls from his room.

"Leftover medley," I answer. He groans, not recalling that it was one of Ruth's expressions. She is still so much with me. She peoples my stories. What she said, how she looked, what she did. To me, with me, for me.

I slit open another envelope and scan the typewritten words. Significant dates and numbers confirm what I already know. Publication slated for October, first-novel interviews, travel schedule. I lay the letter, the measure of my success, aside and read Ruth's note again, perplexed by the reference to *Roman Holiday*. But only momentarily perplexed. Our conversation of movies and motives and mournings as we lay across the bed confronts me word for word across the years and circumstances; across the infinite silence and the bittersweet sadness.

"Oh, honeee," Ruth had said, draining and drawing out the last vowel with theatrical emphasis. "Oh, Pril. Don't you know the best stories are about separation? About partings and leavings?"

"You mean those are the only stories worth writing about?" I'd asked.

"No," she'd said. "I mean those are the only stories there *are*."

And this is mine.